GUN TALK

GUN TALK

CORBA SUNMAN

A Black Horse Western

ROBERT HALE · LONDON

© Corba Sunman 1997
First published in Great Britain 1997

ISBN 0 7090 6086 6

Robert Hale Limited
Clerkenwell House
Clerkenwell Green
London EC1R 0HT

Photoset in North Wales by
Derek Doyle & Associates, Mold, Flintshire.
Printed and bound in Great Britain by
WBC Book Manufacturers Limited,
Bridgend, Mid-Glamorgan.

ONE

Matt Carson reached a fork in the seemingly endless trail he was following and glanced at the signpost. CATTLE CREEK 2 MILES. Population 829. He sighed heavily, his angular face set in grim lines as he touched spurs to his black. The end of his trip was in sight but he was not looking forward to it, and his thoughts had been harsh since the grim news of his brother's death reached him two weeks earlier. Lon, the town marshal of Cattle Creek, had been shot in the back.

The April sun was warm as it shone upon a range slowly awakening from the grip of winter. Carson could feel its heat on his back as he continued westward. He straightened his slumped shoulders. He had taken leave from his job as a deputy U.S. marshal to ride to Cattle Creek in Nevada in response to the anguished message sent him by Lon's widow, Annie, and was filled with a hard resolution to bring his brother's killer to justice.

His right hand dropped to the butt of the Colt .45 holstered on his right hip and he clenched his teeth as emotion speared through him. Gazing ahead, he saw a collection of buildings in the distance. Cattle Creek at last. Tension gripped him as he continued along the dusty trail.

To the right and just before the outskirts of the town his keen gaze picked out the stark vista of the town cemetery, and his pale eyes narrowed as he turned his black towards it. Lon would have been buried two weeks ago, he thought, and anger filled him. By all accounts Cattle Creek was a quiet town, but his brother was dead at thirty-six, and Lon's wife, Annie, and his young son, Joel, had been left alone to fend for themselves.

As he neared the gateway to the cemetery Carson heard a thin voice yelling in sharp protest, and frowned, figuring that someone was in trouble. He heard the sound of rapid hooves just beyond the brow of the hill over which the cemetery stretched, and tensed as he faced the direction from which the sounds emanated. The next moment a smallish figure came into sight, running as if chased by the Devil, and close behind appeared a big man mounted on a chestnut stallion that was doing its best, under the man's guidance, to stomp the running figure into the dust.

Carson reined in quickly, for the running figure almost fell beneath the hooves of his black, and he saw a startled, youthful face looking up at him as a boy dodged sideways and darted behind the black. The rider of the chestnut was coming so fast he had difficulty reining aside, and hauled viciously on his reins to bring the horse to a slithering, dust-raising halt only a foot or two from where Carson sat his mount.

'What the hell!' the man gasped, and Carson

found himself looking into a heavy, black-whiskered face that was grimed and dusty. A long, broken nose jutted as a prominent centre-piece to ugly features, protruding between a thick-lipped, sneering mouth and mean-looking dark eyes that burned with furious intensity. The skin of the face was weatherbeaten, and a network of wrinkles surrounded the eyes.

'What's going on?' demanded Carson.

'What's it to you?' The man was large, with wide shoulders, his tall figure packing heavy muscles and solid flesh.

'Watch out for him, mister,' the boy called urgently from Carson's rear. 'He's Ham Johnson. You get on the wrong side of him and he'll stomp you real bad. I was only looking at my pa's grave, and Johnson figured to have some fun with me. He said he was gonna hang me by my thumbs from that oak tree.'

Carson had pegged Johnson as a bully, and was watching the man closely.

'Try picking on someone your own size,' he said sharply.

'You're big enough.' Johnson's right hand flailed into action, swinging fast to connect with Carson's jaw.

Carson swayed to his left and the clenched fist whirled by his head. He leaned sideways in his saddle and reached for Johnson's right elbow as the man was swung away from him by the force of his blow. Grasping the massive arm, he dragged it back towards him, snaking the fingers of his left hand around Johnson's wrist. He kicked his feet clear of his stirrups and dived over Johnson's horse, maintaining his grip on the man's arm, and the weight of his swiftly moving body dragged the big man out of his saddle. Landing on his feet, Carson released Johnson, who sprawled heavily in the dust, landing on his shoulders and rolling on to his face.

Carson stepped back a couple of paces, watching the fallen man intently, ready for tricks. The next instant Johnson came up out of the dust and lunged forward, snarling in fury as his big hands reached out to grasp Carson. The boy uttered a short cry of warning, but Carson was ready. His right fist sledged up from the region of his hip, perfectly timed, and his hard knuckles smacked against the flesh and bone of Johnson's big jowl. The man's rush was brought up short by the impact and he twisted sideways and went down into the dust again, his face pushing into the dirt. But he was too big and powerful to be disposed of by a single blow and rolled over and lurched to his feet. He paused for a moment to study Carson from under bushy black brows, then grinned and lifted his hands.

'You'll pay for that,' he rasped, and came forward quickly, his big fists held face high and moving in small circles.

Carson threw a straight left that took Johnson in the mouth with the noise of a cracking whip. Blood spurted and Johnson was checked in his stride. Carson loosed a follow-up right that landed on the side of Johnson's jaw. The big man's knees almost gave way and he threw his arms wide to maintain his balance as he staggered. Carson stepped in quickly and jolted his left into the bigger man's solar plexus. Johnson's head came forward, and Carson's right fist flashed to meet it, connecting solidly.

Johnson hit the dirt again, and lay on his back, arms wide, his big chest rising and falling rapidly as he gasped for breath. The boy was cheering Carson at the top of his voice. Johnson rolled over and pushed himself upright, growling in rage.

'I'll kill yuh!' he snarled as he came forward again.

Carson met him with a left as straight as a rifle barrel, timing the punch perfectly. The impact checked Johnson in his stride, but such was his fury he took the blow and kept moving, rampaging like a maddened buffalo, bent on overwhelming this tormenting stranger. His fists whirled and his punches hammered ferociously, but he failed to land a telling blow on the taunting figure that moved before him, always just out of reach and punishing him with heavy blows each time he missed. He lashed out with his feet but Carson was not at the receiving end, moving too swiftly to be caught and smashing home punishing blows that knocked Johnson to the ground again and again.

Johnson's face began to show signs of the treatment he was receiving, his ugly features swelling, his piggish eyes closing, and blood streamed from his nose and cut lips. But he could not admit defeat. and when the message finally began to sink into his animal-like brain his insensate rage pushed him into a different form of action. Hitting the ground again, he rolled and, instead of rushing immediately to his feet, stayed down and clawed for the holstered sixgun on his right thigh.

Carson was expecting such a move and had already flicked off the leather retaining loop on the hammer of his weapon, which held the revolver in its holster. He palmed the big .45 when Johnson reached for his gun, and stood with feet apart and legs braced, his muzzle gaping at Johnson like a malevolent black eye before the big man could clear leather.

'Hold it!' he rapped. 'I figure you've had enough for one day. Let it lie there, mister.'

Johnson could not see clearly through his fist-battered eyes, and blinked at the hazy figure of the man who had bested him. He saw the gun steady in Carson's right hand, cocked and ready for use, and a speck of sanity stabbed into his inflamed mind. He managed to stop the movement of his gunhand, and froze on the brink of death, filled with unaccustomed indecision, his rage spurring him to continue the movement, but he realized that he was staring into hell and thrust his weapon deep into its holster. His hand fell back into the dust and he slumped, his face distorted with fury as he gasped for breath.

'Get up and get the hell outa here,' rasped Carson. 'You better find yourself a new set of ideas, mister. I figure to be around Cattle Creek for a spell, and if I catch you bullying again I'll put you out of circulation real permanent.'

He stepped back a couple of paces and half turned away from the fallen hardcase, holstering his Colt as he did so. But he did not relax, and when the boy yelled a warning he did not need it for he saw the swift movement of Johnson's gunhand snatching at the butt of his gun. He reacted instinctively. Palming his Colt in a blur of speed, he cocked the weapon before it cleared leather, and his trigger finger tensed, firing a single shot when he saw that Johnson was intent on gunning him down. The big weapon blasted raucously and smoke flared, the crash of the shot hammering out the silence and throwing a string of echoes that reverberated hollowly.

Johnson jerked and dropped his gun when the half-inch slug smacked into the fleshy part of his right upper arm. He cried out as pain slashed through him and fell back, grovelling like an animal, sick and beaten, the fight blasted out of him. He groaned and rolled, a tiny flicker of deadly intent bursting into flame in the deeper recesses of his mind as he staggered to his feet. He would not rest until this violent stranger was dead.

'Leave your gun and get the hell outa here,' Carson snapped. 'Mister, you so much as glance in my direction after this and I'll put you six feet under.' He stepped up to Johnson's horse and slid a Winchester 30-30 out of the saddleboot. 'I'll drop your weapons off at the law office in town,' he added. 'But you better be careful around me in future. Now beat it.'

Johnson stared at Carson for interminable moments, his ugly features distorted by rage and the humiliation of defeat. Then he lurched towards his horse, snatched up the trailing reins and dragged himself into the saddle. He moved off slowly, heading towards Cattle Creek, and Carson emitted a sigh as his tension seeped away. He holstered his gun and flexed his hands. His knuckles were bruised, and that was not good for a man whose life often depended on his gun speed.

'That sure was somethin' to see, mister!' the boy declared, his voice tremoring with excitement. 'Ham Johnson makes big tracks around here. I ain't never heard that he was knocked off his feet before, and no one ever bested him with a gun. There are half a dozen men buried here who thought they could beat him.'

Carson looked at the youngster, seeing a boy of around twelve years old, tall and slender like a sapling, his eyes burning with excitement. He was wearing a red shirt, denim trousers and thick shoes, with a small, flat brimmed plains hat perched atop a mass of blond curly hair.

'I'm obliged to you, mister,' the boy continued. 'It was real good of you to step in. Ham Johnson is a bad man, and you took a big chance going against him.'

'Why'd he pick on you?' Carson's weatherbeaten face was set in grim lines. He was tall, standing three inches over six feet, raw-boned and heavily muscled, with narrowed blue eyes and angular features. Clad in dusty range clothes, he had the six-pointed star of a deputy U.S. marshal pinned to his shirt and partially concealed by the leather vest he was wearing, and there was an air about him that should have warned Ham Johnson to be careful. 'You said something about visiting your pa's grave.'

'Pa was the town marshal of Cattle Creek until he was shot dead two weeks ago.' The boy's sad face twisted with anguish.

Carson felt a twinge of emotion at the words, and drew a quick breath.

'You'll be Joel Carson then. And your pa was Lon.' A tugging sensation manifested itself in Carson's breast as he gazed at the boy, whom he had last seen as a babe in arms.

'You bet! And he was the best durned lawman this side of the Great Divide!' The boy paused, then added, 'Apart from my Uncle Matt, that is.' He smiled wistfully. 'Did you know my pa, mister?'

'I sure did!' Carson's blue eyes were filled with an icy expression. 'He was my brother, Joel. I'm Matt Carson.'

'Uncle Matt!' Joel's blue eyes widened. 'Say, you do look a lot like pa at that. Me and ma have been expecting you to show up.'

'And it looks like I turned up just right, huh?' Carson glanced towards the nearby town and saw Johnson disappearing into the wide main street. 'So what's going on round here, Joel? Has your pa's killer been arrested?'

'Nobody knows who did it.' Joel shook his head. 'Pa was found dead in an alley with a bullet in his back. No one even heard the shot. Sheriff Rourke says it's a big mystery.'

'What kind of trouble is there around here?'

'How'd you know there's trouble?' Joel frowned.

'Your pa wouldn't have been killed for nothing.'

Joel nodded. 'There's rustling on the range, and the bank over in Prescott was robbed about a month ago. But Cattle Creek has been as quiet as this place.' He looked around at the rows of wooden crosses. 'You'll want to see pa's grave, huh?'

'Sure.' Carson followed the boy over the crest of the hill on which the cemetery lay, and blinked rapidly when he stood at the foot of a fresh mound of earth looking at the simple wooden cross marking the last resting place of his brother. 'We'll find the man who killed him, Joel,' he said, 'and make him pay for it.'

'One way or another.' The boy nodded. 'I already figured to do the hunting when I get old enough. I've been looking and listening around. And you know what? No one else is bothered. The sheriff rode over from Prescott, the county seat, and looked around but came up with nothing, which ain't surprising seeing he's Barney Rourke. He ain't done a fair day's law dealing in many a long year, so pa said.'

'I reckon your pa found something crooked.'

'And the crooks killed him to shut his mouth!' Joel nodded. 'That's how I got it figured, Uncle Matt.'

'Drop the "Uncle" tag. Call me Matt,' Carson looked down into the boy's intent face, saw the family likeness in its clean lines, and placed a hand on Joel's shoulder. 'Why was Johnson hurrahing you?'

'He's a bully! He picks on anyone who gets in his way.'

'There must be a reason why he picked on you. What does he do around town?'

'He's the sheriff's deputy in Cattle Creek.'

'What!' Carson frowned, then shook his head. 'That could be awkward,' he mused. 'He's some deputy though! I wonder what he does for amusement? Pulls the wings off flies, mebbe?'

'Ma says he's a bad man to cross.'

'Yeah, well we've crossed him. We better get on into town and see your ma, Joel. How's she taking your pa's death?'

'Real bad.' The boy shook his head, his lips compressed. 'She's working in the eating house in town to earn money. We had to leave the house pa had as town marshal, and we're living in a shack across town. I wanted to leave school and take a job, but ma won't let me. Mebbe you can talk some sense into her.'

Carson's gaze lingered on his brother's grave. Then he turned away, and Joel followed him to where the big black was standing with trailing reins. Carson gathered up Johnson's discarded weapons, then glanced at Joel.

'You wanta ride into town?' he asked.

'Yeah!' The boy's eyes shone. 'Pa was fixing to buy me a pony this year.' His voice trailed off as emotion hit him.

Carson shook his head. He boosted Joel into the saddle, soothing the horse as it cavorted nervously, then took hold of the reins and led the animal from the cemetery.

'There's a rider coming from town,' Joel reported.

Carson gazed towards the distant buildings.

'Looks like the sheriff, Barney Rourke,' Joel continued. 'Mebbe Johnson's told him about you, Matt. Rourke might be coming to arrest you.'

'He can try if he likes.' Carson waited for the approaching rider to arrive. He saw a short, heavy figure in the saddle of the nearing horse, and was not impressed by the appearance of the man, who was wearing a five-pointed law badge on his dusty shirt.

Barney Rourke was probably fifty years old, dressed in a crumpled store suit and a greasy black Stetson. He sat slumped on a brown mare, over-weight and, according to Joel, under-active as a lawman. When he arrived he reined up and sat motionless in his saddle, his narrowed brown eyes glinting as he took in Carson's appearance. He looked as if he had not changed his clothes in six months.

'What happened here?' he demanded harshly. 'My deputy just rode into town with a bullet in his arm, and his description of the man who shot him fits you, stranger. Get your hands up. I'm arresting you. You'll see the inside of the jail till I get the straight of what happened.'

'You sure picked yourself one helluva deputy,' Carson observed. 'He was bullying this youngster.' He went on to describe what had happened. 'And how come he doesn't wear a law badge?'

'Johnson might not be everyone's idea of a lawman, but he does his job well enough,' Rourke snapped. 'I ain't seen you in this neck of the woods before, mister. You drifting through or do you got business in town?'

'He's my Uncle Matt, and he's sure got business here,' cut in Joel, pride lacing his thin tone. 'He's gonna find out who killed my pa, which is some-thing you ain't tried to do.'

Carson saw the sheriff's expression harden at Joel's words, and the man's brown eyes narrowed as he scratched his stubbled chin.

'Seems like I got a notice in my office back in Prescott telling me Lon Carson's brother was on his way.' He nodded. 'So you're him! And that notice from the federal marshal told me you're a deputy U.S. marshal and I got to give you whatever help you might need!' Rourke grinned leeringly, and Carson gained the impression that he had walked into trouble, for there was no sign of a welcome in the old lawman's face.

TWO

'I ain't on federal business, Sheriff,' Carson said. 'I got leave of absence to visit my family because my brother is dead, and I was figuring to drop by your office in Prescott to check with you. Finding you here in Cattle Creek saves me a long ride.'

'There ain't anything I can tell you.' Rourke shook his head. 'It's a big mystery why Lon was killed. There ain't been no trouble to speak of in Cattle Creek. Lon hadn't arrested anyone in weeks, so it wasn't a case of someone being sore at him.'

'But someone was sore enough to shoot him in the back,' Carson observed, 'and I'm gonna find him before I'm through around here. I'll see you later, Sheriff, if you're sticking around Cattle Creek. Right now I need to eat and get cleaned up.' He stepped around the lawman's horse and led his black towards the town.

Cattle Creek seemed quiet and unassuming with its six streets and eight hundred or so inhabitants. It served perhaps two dozen big cattle spreads and several hundred nester families on the surrounding range. Carson looked around intently as he paused on the threshold of

19

Main Street, having passed a livery barn, a couple of corrals and a network of stock pens situated on the left. The five minor streets radiated from the hub of Main Street like the spokes of a cartwheel. His keen gaze noted six saloons, a bank, two general stores, a drug store, a barber shop, three restaurants, two hotels, and a brick-built law office and jail among the general run of clap-boarded buildings on the main street. He glanced back at the livery barn.

'I'll take care of your horse, Matt.' Joel slid out of the saddle. 'I help Mr Larter, the liveryman, every Saturday.'

'OK.' Carson reached into his pocket and produced a silver dollar. 'I'll be sticking around for a couple of weeks at least. Give the horse the best, Joel. Where will I find your ma?'

'At the restaurant called the Good Eaterie. It's about halfway along the street on the right from here. Ma'll be real busy now it's be supper time.'

'I need to get a bite to eat,' Carson mused. 'Join me there when you get through with the horse.'

'I sure will!' Joel smiled but his eyes were sad.

Carson took his saddlebags from behind the cantle and flung them across his left shoulder, then drew his .45-.70 from its saddle boot and carried it in the crook of his left arm.

'I'll rent a room in the hotel and dump this stuff before I look up your ma,' he said. 'See you later, Joel.'

He walked along the main street towards the hotel, and as he passed Kunkel's General Store a large, ruddy-faced man some fifty years old appeared in the doorway. He looked fat and sleek

from good living, and an aura of prosperity emanated from him. His white hair was slicked down,
his shirt sleeves neatly rolled to the elbows, and his
white apron was spotless despite the lateness of
the hour.

Carson took in the man's appearance without
seeming to glance in his direction, and did not
break his step, but the storekeeper called to him
and Carson halted, keen to learn what he could of
the local situation.

'Evenin', stranger.' There was a faint trace of
guttural accent in the man's voice. 'Looks like
you've ridden far.'

Carson nodded. 'Yeah, and then some.'

'Are you the man who shot Ham Johnson?'

Carson nodded again. 'News sure travels fast in
this place,' he observed. 'It's a pity there's nothing
going the rounds about my brother's murder.'

'So you're Matt Carson!'

Carson studied the storekeeper's fleshy face.
'You seem to know a lot. So who killed my brother?'

'I am sorry. That is a complete mystery. Only one
man knows for sure who did the killing.'

'And that'll be the killer, huh? Well I guess that
figures. But I aim to change all that now I'm here.
Who are you?'

'Otto Kunkel at your service. I own this store.
Everyone knows "Uncle Otto". I am also the town
mayor, and I am concerned about the trouble
building up around here. I heard tell that you are a
deputy U.S. marshal.'

'Yeah. I'm not here officially but I sure mean to
look into Lon's death. I guess you knew my brother
well, huh?'

'Very well. It is a tragedy that such a man should be cut down in the prime of his life, and I hope the killer will be found. If there's anything I can do to help you then let me know.'

'What I need is information,' Carson replied. 'And I figure you're the man to give it to me. Storekeepers get to hear all the talk going the rounds.'

'Gossip won't help you find the killer.' Kunkel shook his head. 'You need facts, and I can't supply those.'

'You spoke of trouble coming around here. Tell me about that. The men responsible might lead me to Lon's killer.'

'There's nothing I can put my finger on, and it wouldn't help to learn the gossip. It might throw you off the right trail.'

'I disagree. Lon might have got wind of the trouble you're talking about and stepped on the toes of those responsible. But if you're afraid to speak I'll have to do this the hard way.'

Kunkel opened his mouth to protest but Carson turned away abruptly and continued to the nearby hotel. After booking a room, he paid the attentive clerk, who gazed intently at his signature in the hotel register. Carrying his gear up to his room, he washed up and changed his shirt, then beat the worst of the dust from his clothes. He took the trouble to clean his gun before leaving the room, and when he reached the lobby there were several men standing at the desk, chatting eagerly with the clerk.

'I tell you he's got to be Lon Carson's brother!' the clerk was saying.

'Come to find Lon's killer,' suggested another.

Carson ignored them and went out to the sidewalk. The sun was well over in the western half of the sky and heat was packing the town. There was a breeze, but it was hot. He glanced around the street. A couple of dance hall girls were standing in the doorway of a tall building almost opposite, and several others were lounging on a balcony above them. One of the girls waved to Carson, and he smiled and let his gaze move on. His expression sobered when he saw the law office to the right, and wondered how many times Lon had gone in and out of the place over the last ten years.

He walked along the street to the restaurant and entered. Most of the small tables were occupied, but he found one vacant in a corner near the kitchen and sat down. A girl was hurrying around serving the customers, her perspiring face flushed. She was rather tight-lipped, Carson observed, and pointedly ignoring the remarks thrown at her by the male diners crowding the place. Carson relaxed and looked around, trying to gauge the general mood of these men. If there was trouble in this town then there would be tension among its inhabitants.

After a few moments the waitress reached Carson's table and lifted her pad and pencil expectantly.

'Is Annie Carson around?' he asked.

'She's busy in the kitchen. Who wants to know?' The girl's keen gaze rested momentarily on his lean features.

'I'm Matt Carson. Annie's husband was my brother.'

The girl subjected Carson to an intent gaze. Then she nodded and her expression became animated. 'I can see the resemblance,' she said curtly. 'I'll tell Annie you're here. She's been expecting you to ride in. Do you need some food?'

'A big steak with all the trimmings, and apple pie.'

'You'll get the biggest and the best,' she responded. 'I'm sure glad to see you. Someone's got to do something about the way Lon was killed and there ain't no one hereabouts who's prepared to stick his neck out.'

Carson nodded. 'I'll do my best to uncover it.'

The girl hurried away to push through a door in the back wall. Carson watched the door, and a moment later Annie emerged, looking around eagerly. He lifted a hand to attract her attention and got to his feet when she came to his corner.

'Matt, I'm so glad to see you!' She grasped his hand. 'I'm sorry I can't stop now. We're so busy. But I'll be through here in about an hour.'

'That's OK.' He squeezed her hand. 'I'm gonna have supper, and Joel will be joining me shortly. We'll wait for you.'

'You've seen Joel?' Annie was tall and slender, with dark eyes and soft brown hair drawn loosely back from a rounded forehead. Her features were finely chiselled.

'He was at the cemetery.' Carson said no more, but Annie drew back, her face expressing fear.

'There's talk that Ham Johnson ran into more trouble than he could handle out at the cemetery. Were you involved, Matt?'

'Some.' His harsh features did not relax. 'It ain't

nothing to talk about.'

'They say Johnson was shot and his face badly bruised.'

'I reckon he didn't get more than he asked for.'

'Be very careful, Matt! They killed Lon, and they wouldn't hesitate to do the same to you if they thought you planned to horn in on their play.'

'We can talk later, and perhaps you can give me the lowdown on what's been happening around here.'

'I'm afraid there's not much I can tell you. All I do know is that Lon was convinced trouble was coming. That much he told me. But I don't think he knew anything for certain.'

'He must have learned something because he was killed!' Carson shook his head. 'Or they figured he knew something. But don't worry. We'll get down to it later, Annie.'

She nodded and returned to the kitchen. Carson dropped back into his seat and sat thinking about his brother. When his meal arrived he ate it reflectively, hardly aware of what was on his plate. Then Joel joined him, slipping into a seat opposite, and Carson looked up with a quick smile.

'You need something to eat, Joel?' he demanded.

'Ma will send my supper out when Martha sees me here.' The youngster's expression hardened. 'I just seen Johnson on the street with his sidekick, Shap Newman. The two of them had their heads together talking turkey. I tried to get close and hear what they were saying but they spotted me and moved on. I figure they was talking about you, Matt. You got to walk careful now.'

'Is Newman also a deputy?' Carson asked.

'Nope.' Joel grimaced. 'He's the new town marshal.'

'I reckon, by your tone, that Newman is a man like Johnson, huh?'

'Worse. He's bigger and harder than Johnson. How they came to pick him to be the town lawman beats me, Matt.'

'Otto Kunkel is the town mayor. He would have had a hand in giving Newman the town marshal's job.'

'You know Kunkel? He owns the big store, the livery, and the blacksmith's.' Joel broke off as the waitress appeared, bringing coffee for Carson and supper for Joel.

Carson recalled the big man he had seen standing in the doorway of the store. So Kunkel had a large slice of the business in Cattle Creek. He blinked, his instincts already at work. Someone with his experience could soon get to the root of what had been going on around here. It was all a matter of seeking motives and checking up on the various circles of association existing within the town. Someone had elected the new town marshal, and if Newman was as bad as Joel suggested then there had to be a good reason, or a bad one, for the man's appointment.

'There's Shap Newman now,' Joel whispered as the street door banged loudly.

Carson looked over the rim of his coffee cup and saw a great hulk of a man standing on the threshold. He was deep in the chest and had massive shoulders. His features were beefy, and so large that his cheeks and jowl swelled into a continuous line of bulging flesh. He was dressed in a dark store suit that seemed one size too small, and crossed cartridge belts sagged around his waist, supporting dark, greased holsters containing a matching pair of pearlhandled sixguns. A five-pointed star was pinned to his shirt front.

'He don't look to be an improvement on Johnson,' Carson observed.

Joel laughed, the sound ringing out across the big dining room. Heads turned in their direction, and Carson, watching Newman closely, met the man's glance. Newman was scowling, his dark eyes glinting, and his right hand dropped to the butt of his holstered gun. He remained motionless for several moments, then turned away and sat at a table in the opposite corner.

'He comes in here every night about this time,' Joel said. 'Frank Brice owns this place, and I think he's scared of Newman. Every night Newman gets a free supper, but my pa was the town marshal for ten years and always had to pay.'

Carson sipped his coffee. 'Was Newman around while your pa was alive?' he asked.

'I can't say for sure when he showed up, but he wasn't around before Pa was killed. I think he rode in a couple of days afterwards.'

Carson finished his coffee and set down the cup. Joel was eating his supper. Carson pushed back his chair.

'Finish your supper and wait here until your ma gets through. I figure to look around the town and set the landmarks in my mind. I'll come back before this place closes.'

'Don't take any chances, Matt.' Joel spoke quietly, his youthful face tense. 'You made a bad enemy of Ham Johnson, and him being what he is, you could have big trouble on your hands.'

'Don't worry about me.' Carson got to his feet, smiling. 'I can take care of myself, Joel.'

'Yeah.' The boy nodded grimly. 'I recall that's what Pa used to say when Ma told him to be careful, and now he's dead. So watch your back, huh?'

Carson placed a silver coin on the table beside his plate. 'Tell the waitress to keep the change,' he said, and departed.

He was aware that all eyes marked his progress to the door, and a sigh escaped him when he reached the sidewalk. The breeze had lost much of its fire, he discovered. The sun was now low in the west, reaching down for the peaks on the horizon, and the sky was a glory of red-gold fire. Carson drew a deep breath and held it for a moment, looking around intently, his keen gaze searching every dusty corner of his surroundings.

If he had arrived here three weeks ago he would have found his brother still alive. The remote thought rode through his mind. Such a short time, but it could not be recalled, and instead of seeing Lon he had to face the grim chore of finding his brother's killer. He forced his thoughts into the background and strode along the sidewalk towards the law office. He had to make a start, and the sooner the better. Someone in Cattle Creek knew what was going on, and there was only one way to get at the truth. It would be difficult and dangerous to root out the facts but he relished the thought that he might soon be in action against Lon's killer.

Shadows were creeping in around the wide street as he crossed to the law office, where yellow lamplight was already spilling out through the big window overlooking the sidewalk. He paused at the door of the office and glanced around the street. A furtive movement in an alley mouth almost opposite caught his attention and he dropped a hand to his holstered gun, ready to flow into action. He saw the shadowy outline of a figure standing half hidden at the corner of the alley opposite, and it eased back out of sight when it realized that it had been seen. Carson frowned as he entered the office.

Sheriff Rourke was seated at a large, untidy desk, eating supper, and he peered up at Carson from under dark, bushy brows. He nodded, his mouth filled with food, his jaw champing like a horse eating hay. He swallowed, put down his knife and fork, and pushed his plate aside.

'Taking a look around town, huh?' he commented. 'It ain't much to look at, and most of these folk are good people.'

'That figures.' Carson nodded. 'But it ain't the good folk I'm interested in so tell me about the not so good. And you can start with your deputy. What kind of a man is Johnson? I came up with him in the cemetery trying to stomp young Joel and he attacked me for no good reason. When I taught him a lesson with my fists he tried to draw on me.'

'Ham has a strange sense of humour and plays rough.' Rourke shrugged, his face expressionless. 'But he's a good lawman.'

'And you rode out to the cemetery to arrest me on his say-so,' Carson continued.

'I came out to check up on what happened.'

'I told you, and, being a deputy U.S. marshal, my word will stand in any court of law, so what did you do when you came back to town? Is Johnson behind bars?'

'No.' Rourke shook his head. 'You didn't make a charge. I follow the letter of the law, Carson. Do you wanta charge him?'

'I figure he should be behind bars, and if the way he handled me is a sample of how he runs the law then his badge should be taken away. I'll make charges against him. Where is he?'

'The doc patched him up and he's taken to his bed for a few days.' Rourke's craggy face was expressionless.

'Jail him tomorrow and I'll make the necessary charge. Now let's get down to my brother's murder. What can you tell me?'

'Only the facts.' Rourke shrugged. 'Lon was making his last round of the day. His killer was waiting in the alley between Kunkel's store and the bank. Lon entered the alley and was shot in the back. I investigated but didn't turn up anything. All I found were boot marks in the alley where the killer had run for a horse waiting on the back lots after the shooting. Lon died instantly and there were no witnesses. That's all I have. I came over from Prescott soon as I got word of what happened and I've been here ever since. I spent a lot of time going over the business and came up with nothing.'

Carson nodded. 'That's no more than I expected.

So what's going on around here? What trouble do you have?'

'Nothing that can point to Lon's murder. There's a bit of rustling on the range, but being the town marshal, it wasn't any part of Lon's job so he wasn't involved. The town's been quiet for months. Lon didn't have any kind of a run-in with anyone, and there ain't been no hardcases passing through lately. The murder is a mystery, and nothing has come to light about it.'

Carson turned away, aware that if there was any evidence he would not get it from the local law department.

'What about the new town marshal?' he queried. 'Where did he come from, and how did he get the job?'

'Newman turned up a few days after Lon died, and he came with a big reputation. He was a town lawman down in Texas.'

'Did you check on him?'

'Sure. Sent a wire to the sheriff of Pearson County, Texas, who confirmed everything Newman told us. I figure we was lucky to get a man like Newman so soon after losing Lon.'

Carson moved to the door. 'I'll spend a few days looking around,' he said quietly. 'I'll see you in the morning and swear out charges against Johnson. He ain't fit to wear a badge.'

'If you say so.' Rourke nodded. 'It goes without saying that I'm ready to help you any way I can. But I'll be going back to Prescott any day now. I got other matters to handle, and I'm getting nowhere fast with your brother's murder.'

Carson nodded and departed. Closing the street

door, he stood on the sidewalk looking around, his thoughts busy. He went along the sidewalk to the nearest saloon, needing a drink, and as he passed a lighted lamp set on the front wall of the saloon a gun crashed in the nearby shadows with startling suddenness. A bullet struck the lamp, shattering it and extinguishing the light. The slug came within an inch of hitting Carson in the head, and before the echoes of the shot could roll away he was down in the dust in front of the sidewalk, sixgun in his hand, his narrowed blue eyes searching for the ambusher.

So this was the way it was going to be. The same as it had been for Lon. Something was seriously wrong around this quiet little town, and it would have to be put right, the hard way.

THREE

Carson narrowed his eyes as he probed the shadows. The echoes of the shot were fading into the distance, and he sprang up and dashed across the rutted street towards the alley mouth where the gun flash had winked and died. His Colt was levelled in his right hand, cocked and ready for action, and his muscles were tensed as he anticipated a second shot.

He reached the alley mouth without incident and paused to peer into the impenetrable darkness concealing it. At that moment he heard a rapid tattoo of hooves from the back lots, and sighed heavily to disperse his tension. This was what had happened to Lon – a shot fired out of the darkness of an alley and the killer riding away over the back lots. He realized that he had no chance of catching his attacker and returned his gun to its holster.

Standing in the shadows of the alley mouth, he peered around the street. Men were emerging from the saloon, and a couple of figures appeared from the opposite ends of the street, walking into the lamplight and reaching the sidewalk in front of batwings at about the same time. One was

Sheriff Rourke and the other was the new town marshal, Shap Newman. Carson wondered if Newman had come straight from the eating house, but realized that the man could not have shot at him, ridden away, then arrived here so quickly.

He moved noiselessly along the sidewalk opposite the saloon, sneaking away into the darkness, not wanting the fact that he had been shot at to become public knowledge. At least he had proof now that whoever killed Lon was still in the locality and afraid that details of the murder would be exposed.

He returned to the eating house and entered, pushing through the little knot of diners standing on the sidewalk talking about the disturbance. Annie was inside, her face strained with fear, but she brightened when he entered, and came towards him.

'Are you OK, Matt?' she demanded. 'When I heard the shot it reminded me of Lon. I sent Joel to find out what happened.'

'I wasn't involved.' Carson wanted to allay her fears, and at that moment Joel returned, his expression grim. When he saw Carson a smile came to his face.

'There's a big crowd along the street,' he reported. 'Someone shot out a lamp in front of the saloon. No one was hurt.'

The diners were beginning to file back into the building to return to their interrupted meal. Newman appeared, scowling, and sat down at the corner table to resume eating as if nothing had disturbed him.

'Was Newman sitting over there when the shot

was fired?' Carson asked.

'Yeah,' Joel answered. 'He got off his chair like greased lightning, rushed out the door, and ran along the boardwalk.'

'Where does Ham Johnson hit the sack when he's not on duty?' Carson's thoughts were moving rapidly.

'He's got a shack down by the livery barn,' Joel said.

'Show me,' Carson invited.

'Sure thing!' Joel's eyes gleamed at the thought of more action.

Annie opened her mouth as if to protest but saw the grim expression on Carson's face and shook her head as Joel hurried to the street door with Carson following closely. When they reached the sidewalk Carson dropped a hand to the boy's shoulder.

'Take it easy,' he advised. 'I don't wanta advertise our movements. Tell me, Joel, why was Johnson hurrahing you at the cemetery?'

'No particular reason, I guess. I ain't never done anything to rile him. I was just standing by Pa's grave when he rode up and started bad-mouthing me. When I answered back he spurred his horse at me and I started running. I was sure glad to see you! Johnson is mean and there's no telling how far he'll go.'

'He's sure something else as a lawman, huh?' Carson was watching their surroundings closely, afraid of more shooting while Joel was with him. 'Is he the only deputy in town?'

'Yeah. He's the deputy sheriff. Newman is the town marshal. Between them they run the law around here. The sheriff is only over from Prescott because Pa was killed.'

They reached the livery barn without incident, and Joel headed for the alley to the left. Carson put a hand on the boy's shoulder and restrained him. 'I'll go on alone from here,' he said firmly. 'You go back to your mother now, huh?'

'OK.' Disappointment was plain in Joel's voice. 'Johnson's place is down the alley and straight across the back lots.'

'How far?'

'About fifty yards. You can't miss it.'

'Thanks. Stay in the eating house until I show up.'

The boy turned away reluctantly and Carson entered the alley. The shadows were intense but he could see sufficiently to note his surroundings and reached the back lots, where he paused to look around. There were several buildings out back, and some of them had lamplight in their windows. He selected the one straight ahead and moved carefully over the back lots.

He was still several yards out from the shack when a movement at its front right corner attracted his attention and he halted in midstride. A figure passed the lighted window on its way to the door. Carson palmed his sixgun as the door was opened, and moved in on a big figure as it entered the shack.

Jabbing his gun muzzle against the man's spine, Carson followed him into the shack. The man did not speak and lifted his hands into the air. Carson saw it was Ham Johnson and let his narrowed gaze take in the musty interior of the little building. It was sparsely furnished, with a single bed in a corner.

'Been out for some night air, Johnson?' Carson queried, reaching for the big deputy's holstered gun.

'Yeah. What's it to you?' came the hoarse reply.

Carson snaked Johnson's revolver out of its holster and sniffed at the muzzle. It reeked of burned powder, and he stuffed the weapon into the waistband of his pants.

'You fired a shot at me about five minutes ago when I was in front of the saloon,' observed Carson.

'You're loco. I've been out for a drink.'

'Your gun has been fired recently, and there's been one shot fired in town this evening, with me as the target. I was gonna have you put in jail tomorrow for attacking me in the cemetery, but tonight will do instead. The charge is attempted murder.'

'You got the wrong man,' protested Johnson.

'You picked on the wrong man,' Carson responded, 'unless you figured to kill a deputy U.S. marshal and get away with it. What was your motive? And don't tell me it was because we had that run-in at the cemetery. I wanta know why you attacked me out there in the first place, you being a deputy sheriff an' all.'

'I didn't know who you were,' protested Johnson, lowering his massive arms. He turned to face Carson, his battered features attempting to express innocence. 'All I knew was that you were a stranger and horning in on my business.'

'Why were you giving young Joel a hard time?'

'There's been reports of youngsters causin' damage to some of the graves in the cemetery, and when I caught him out there I figured he was responsible. I was only doing my duty.'

'And shooting at me from cover was also your duty, huh?' Carson shook his head. 'You're a poor excuse for a deputy, Johnson. Come on, you're heading for jail, and you better come up with better reasons for your actions when you face your trial. Ambushing a federal lawman is a serious offence. You'll go to prison for a long time.'

Johnson scowled. 'I was only doing my job,' he snarled.

'Save it for the court,' Carson rapped. 'Let's go.'

He remained alert when they left the shack, staying a couple of feet behind Johnson, his gun levelled at the big deputy's massive back. They reached the sidewalk, and moved on towards the jail. There was still a knot of townsmen standing in front of the saloon, and Sheriff Rourke was there. Carson was pleased because he wanted Johnson's arrest to be known.

'What's going on?' Rourke demanded. His face was gaunt in the lamplight spilling through the saloon windows.

'I've arrested Johnson.' Carson spoke loudly. 'I caught him sneaking into his shack, and when I checked his gun it smelled of gunsmoke.' He drew the big deputy's Colt from his waistband and held it out to the sheriff. 'That's Johnson's gun. Sniff the barrel. There's been one shot fired in town since I arrived, and it came from this weapon.'

'This is Johnson's gun,' observed the sheriff. He sniffed at the muzzle then looked at Johnson. 'And it's been fired recently. What's the story, Johnson?'

Carson looked around at the intent faces of the townsmen, who were gazing silently at Johnson, awaiting the big deputy's explanation. Johnson shrugged and remained silent, and, when it became obvious that he was not going to answer, Carson put a hand to the man's massive shoulder and pushed him towards the jail.

'Silence is as good as a confession,' he observed. 'On your way, Johnson. You know where the jail is. Take him in, Sheriff. I'll charge him in the morning.'

Rourke hefted Johnson's sixgun, and for a moment Carson thought the lawman was going to disobey his instruction. But Rourke nodded.

'He'll be in jail in the morning when you want him,' he said harshly. 'Let's go, Johnson.'

Carson heaved a sigh as the pair moved on along the sidewalk. He had Johnson dead to rights, but needed proof of the man's misdeeds, and figured the only way he could learn anything was by talking to townsmen. He pushed through the knot of men and shouldered his way between the batwings into the saloon, and as he walked to the bar the townsmen followed him, talking loudly.

'It was on the cards that Johnson would overstep the mark one day,' someone remarked.

'Yeah, he's been making big tracks ever since he hit town. He ain't nothing but a bully, but he sure picked on the wrong man when he decided to take you on, Marshal.' A tall, well-dressed man detached himself from the crowd and walked behind the bar. He turned to face the crowd surrounding Carson. Past middle-age, his lean face was wrinkled around the eyes, his dark hair greying at the temples. 'I'm Ash Norton, Marshal. I own this place, and anything you drink in here will be on the house. It's about time Johnson was taken down a peg or two and there was no one around who could do the job until you showed up.'

'Thanks. I could do with a beer,' responded Carson.

Norton slid a foaming schooner of beer along the bar with practised ease. His dark eyes were gleaming as he wiped his hands on a cloth. His store suit was finely cut, well fitting, and there was a jewelled stickpin in his cravat which glinted and sparkled in the lamplight.

'You're Lon Carson's brother, huh?' Norton continued, and leaned his elbows on the bar. 'You sure look like him. His death was a tragedy, Marshal. Lon was well liked around here. He always did his job according to the letter of the law, and nobody stepped out of line when he was on duty. It was a big shock to everyone when he was shot. I sure hope you can get a lead on his killer. The businessmen of the town have put up five hundred dollars reward for information leading to the killer's arrest.'

'Lon was that well-liked, huh?' Carson nodded. 'Has anyone any idea why he was murdered?'

'There were no hardcases in town at the time.' A small man spoke at Carson's side. He was old, dressed in black broadcloth. His blue eyes seemed filled with a spiritual weariness but his voice was sharp. 'I'm Frank Hayman MD.'

'Glad to know you.' Carson's pale eyes were narrowed. 'Did you attend Lon when he was shot?'

'I did. I was one of the first to reach him. He died instantly, shot in the back.'

'Did you remove the bullet?'

The doctor frowned, his eyes narrowing as he considered. Then he shook his head. 'No, I didn't think it mattered. Lon was dead and that was the end of it as far as I was concerned.'

'What was the verdict at the inquest?'

'Murder by a person or persons unknown.' Hayman shrugged. 'There was no evidence anywhere.'

'And everyone is saying there were no strangers in the town at that time,' mused Carson. 'That tells us something.'

'What's that?' Norton demanded.

'A local man must have killed Lon.'

There was shocked silence at Carson's words, and he looked around at the assembled men, taking in their expressions.

'That's a fact that has been overlooked.' Doc Hayman shook his head.

'Which makes the bullet that killed Lon mighty important,' Carson persisted.

'You figure I should have the body exhumed and the bullet recovered?' Hayman nodded. 'Of course. If the bullet turns out to be of an unusual calibre it could prove something.'

'Perhaps you'll arrange for it to be done,' Carson said. 'I'd sure like to examine that slug.'

'I'll get an order from the coroner in the morning,' the doctor said firmly.

Carson drank his beer and set down the glass.

'Thanks for your help,' he said. 'I'll check with you in the morning. Right now I got some things to do.'

He departed, leaving quickly, and a buzz of excited chatter followed him. He reached the sidewalk and sidestepped into the shadows beside the batwings, his narrowed gaze instinctively checking his surroundings. There was little he could do to locate his brother's killer beyond digging into the recent past. But Lon's death could not be motiveless. There had to be a reason, and all he had to do was find it.

He went along the sidewalk to the restaurant, now almost empty of customers, and found Shap Newman, the new town marshal, standing just inside, chatting with the waitress. The girl looked at Carson with relief in her eyes and took the opportunity to hurry away. Carson confronted Newman and looked into the man's eyes, his own expressionless, his face set in harsh lines.

'I guess you know who I am, huh?' asked Carson.

'Sure. Word gets around town pretty fast. I hope you get the man who killed your brother.' Newman's voice was lowpitched, expressionless. 'I can't help. I didn't show up around here until after the murder.'

'So I heard,' Carson nodded. 'Have you come across anything unusual since you took over as town marshal?'

'Such as?'

'Any fact that could throw some light on Lon's death.'

'Nobody's come up and told me who did the shooting, if that's what you mean.' Newman shrugged his heavy shoulders. 'I'm still feeling my way into this job. Folks don't know me well enough yet to trust me.'

'You made friends with Ham Johnson?'

'Nope. I don't like his manner. He ain't my idea of a lawman. I have to mix with him because of my job.'

Carson nodded. 'I've just put Johnson in jail. That shot you heard a short time ago was fired at me, and Johnson did it.'

A glimmer of some undefinable expression showed momentarily in Newman's dark eyes and he nodded. 'I thought he'd overstep the mark one day. Have you got him cold?'

'Yeah,' Carson nodded.

'That's good. You've made a start, which is the important thing. If you need help any time then call out for me. I aim to keep this town clean. Your brother did a good job, and he left me a high standard to live up to.'

'Have you considered that you stepped into a dead man's boots, and wondered why he was killed?' Carson demanded.

'I can't say I have.' Newman shook his head. 'What are you getting at?'

'What happened to the previous town marshal could happen to the present one. You better take all the precautions.'

'Yeah, I see what you mean,' Newman nodded. 'I never take chances, Marshal, but thanks for pointing out the danger. I'm watching my back, you can bet.' He pulled on his black Stetson and prepared to leave. 'I got the last round of the town to make. So long, and call me if you need anything.'

'Thanks,' Carson nodded. What he really needed at this time was a definite clue to Lon's killer. He shook his head, aware that nothing would fall easily into his lap. He had to start digging, and deeply, before anything would happen.

FOUR

Carson was thoughtful as he walked Annie and Joel home. He had questions to ask, and was aware that they would be painful for his brother's widow. But they had to be answered, and the sooner the better.

'You've made an unfortunate start to your visit here, Matt,' Annie said. She had been silent since leaving the restaurant, and now turned to him, her face shadowed in the dim light of a nearby lantern.

'I was thinking I'd made a good start,' he countered. 'I've put a bullying lawman behind bars, and I have a feeling his attack on me is somehow connected with Lon's death.'

'Lon always said he didn't trust Johnson.'

'Did he say why? I need to know everything Lon thought about in the weeks before he died. He would have talked to you, Annie. You probably know more about the background to this business than anyone, but it may not be obvious, so anything you can remember could be helpful.'

'It's all mixed up in my head.' Her voice tremored. 'I've thought about nothing else, trying to work out what happened and who might have

killed Lon. He often said there was badness
beneath the surface of town life, but whenever I
questioned him about it he said I didn't need to
know about such things.' She shook her head
sadly. 'I wish now I'd been more persistent. I
might have learned something.'

They walked on almost to the edge of town, and
Carson peered around at the motley collection of
small buildings. Joel ran on ahead to enter a
small shack, and a moment later yellow lamplight
flared at the small window.

'Lon did say, when he heard about the bank in
Prescott being robbed, that he wasn't surprised it
happened. He mentioned Cal Mabry, who has the
CM cattle spread about ten miles to the west of
town and employs a rough crew. Lon thought
Mabry might know about the bank robbery, but
when he mentioned it to Rourke the sheriff
laughed at him. It's a three-day ride to Prescott
from here, and Rourke said there are witnesses
who saw Mabry here in Cattle Creek at the time
the bank was robbed in Prescott.'

'I'm uneasy about the way Rourke seems to be
handling the law around here,' Carson mused.
'Lon kept a pretty good town, I know, but there
has to be something that will give us a lead to why
he was killed. There's got to be a motive, and I
need to find it. Did anything happen around town
that gave Lon any trouble?'

'Once or twice he said he thought some of the
businessmen in town were in some kind of
trouble.' Annie heaved a sigh. 'I wish he'd told me
more about his work.'

'What about town gossip?'

'There are some men around town Lon did not trust. Ash Norton, the saloonman, is one. Thinking about it, Lon always felt that Norton was the type who would ride roughshod over anyone to get what he wanted.'

Carson nodded. 'Annie, think about what Lon used to tell you, and tomorrow you can give me a run-down.'

'Something comes to mind that I have seen for myself,' she responded. 'I don't know if it means anything, but Frank Brice, who runs the restaurant where I work, seems to be having trouble with the new town marshal.'

'Joel told me that Newman doesn't pay for his meals.'

'That's right. And Johnson is another free-loader. Frank is very worried. I know he hates Johnson, and he's scared of Newman. It's all happened since Newman came to town. Before then, Lon kept everything and everyone in order.'

'Uhuh! Maybe I'll have a chat with Brice. How long has Johnson been a deputy?'

Annie shook her head as she considered. 'He first showed up about a year ago. Sheriff Rourke was out on the range checking on rustling, and had a run-in with some badmen. Johnson showed up and helped him out, so Rourke made him a deputy and stuck him here in Cattle Creek.'

Carson frowned. 'I'll see you in the morning, Annie,' he mused. 'I need to take a closer look around town now.'

'Be careful, Matt. Lon's killer must still be around, and if he figgers you might uncover something about him he wouldn't hesitate to make a try for you.'

Carson smiled. 'That's what I'm hoping will happen! It's the quickest way I can get the deadwood on the killer. When that shot was fired at me I thought I was in luck. But the run-in I had with Johnson might have been the reason why he took that shot at me. If it had been someone else then I could have been in business.'

'You're hoping to be ambushed?' Horror sounded in Annie's voice. She clutched at his arm. 'Don't take any chances, Matt. There's nothing you can do about a bullet in the back.'

'Lon couldn't do anything because he wasn't expecting it,' he retorted grimly. 'But I'm ready for it, and I won't take any chances. See you in the morning.'

He turned away and went back along the street, his big figure a flitting shadow that blended easily with the darkness. Annie watched until he vanished, then sighed and entered the shack.

Carson went back to the restaurant. There were no diners now, and a short, thickset, balding man, looking hot and bothered, was mopping the floor. All the chairs were stacked on the small tables, and Carson paused on the threshold.

'We're closed,' said the man, not pausing in his work.

'I ate earlier. I'm Matt Carson. Lon was my brother.'

'Is that a fact?' The man paused and leaned on his longhandled mop. 'I'm Frank Brice. I own this place. It was a bad thing that happened to Lon. He was a good lawman, and kept things quiet around here.'

'How do you get on with the man who took his place?'

'Newman?' Brice looked up at Carson and shook his head. 'I don't see much of him.'

'But you give him free meals, which is something you didn't do for Lon.'

'Who told you about that?'

Carson shrugged. 'You're scared of something, Brice. I can see it in your manner. And I'll bet you didn't have any worries when Lon ran the town.'

'Lon is dead now.'

'You got any idea who killed him?'

'Nope. I mind my business. I don't see or hear anything. Sure, there's something going on, but it ain't my concern. I work hard for my living, and pay my way. I don't know nothing from nothing, and it's safer that way.'

'So why is Newman free-loading?'

'It's a business arrangement. I feed him and he keeps a special watch on this place. It's the way most other businesses in town handle it, I guess. These are lawless times, and a man has to protect what he's got or lose it.'

'You never had any trouble when Lon was around, huh?'

'Nope. He was a straightshooter. But he's gone, and a wise man takes all the precautions he can.'

'Are you paying money as well?' Carson watched Brice as he asked the question, and saw the man's expression tighten.

'There are some things a man can't talk about.' Brice shook his head.

'Give me proof and I'll act on it.'

'And if you get shot in the back, where would

that leave me?' Brice grimaced. 'I got to live here, Marshal.'

'I'll take your answer to mean you are paying protection, and I'll throw Newman in jail on your say-so.'

'Then have me stand up in court and admit it publicly, huh?' Brice laughed cynically. 'I ain't got no confidence in the law. You arrest Newman on my say-so, then stop a slug, and I'm way out on a limb.'

'There's only one way to end that kind of thing,' Carson insisted, 'and you don't have to stand up and admit it in the first place. I'll get the deadwood on those involved before I arrest them.'

'No.' Brice spoke emphatically. 'My recipe for a good life is live and let live.'

'That's OK as far as it goes, but Lon is no longer living so your rule doesn't work.'

'But I'm still alive, and I wanta keep it that way!'

'So you have been threatened. Well that figures. It's how the racket works. But the minute someone makes a stand against it the whole things folds. It feeds on fear and secrecy, so make a public stand and your problems will fade away.'

'Prove you can make the law work and I'll stand up and be counted,' Brice said doggedly, 'but I ain't sticking my neck out alone.'

'Do you know who else is paying protection?'

'Just about everyone, I guess, but nobody will admit it.'

Carson turned away, and was thoughtful as he went out to the sidewalk. He walked along the street towards the livery barn, keeping to the shadows and moving slowly, nerves hair-triggered, his mind alert to his surroundings.

There was a lantern alight in the livery office just inside the entrance to the barn and Carson loosened his gun in its holster as he eased through the shadows. For some moments he stood just outside the circle of light issuing from the lantern, his gaze probing the surrounding darkness and shadows. He heard a horse stamping inside the barn but there were no other sounds in the night.

He looked into the dusty office and saw a man dozing at the desk, head in his hands. Rapping softly on the open door, Carson saw the man open his eyes.

'Howdy,' he greeted. 'I'm Matt Carson.'

'Howdy. Heard you was in town. I'm Frank Larter. Glad to meet you. Joel told me about you when he brought your horse in. It was a bad business about Lon. He was a good man.'

Larter got to his feet, a tall, thin, oldish man with a seamed, weatherbeaten face and a straggly, greying moustache.

'You see all the comings and goings around town,' Carson mused. 'Is there anything you can tell me about the night Lon was killed? Was there anything unusual about it?'

'I don't see anything that goes on around town.' Larter shook his head. 'I'm stuck in this place sixteen hours a day, seven days a week. I can recognise every horse in the county and tell you who it belongs to, but anything happening around town comes to me only if somebody talks about it.'

'What's the general talk around town about Lon's death?'

'Nobody knows anything. Everyone is asking the same question. Who killed him? The town had been peaceful since Lon took over. He stopped all the brawling and shootings. He made it safe for women and children to live in.'

'How'd he get along with Ham Johnson?'

'Lon didn't like Johnson. Nobody likes Johnson! Him and Lon were like two bulls in the same stockyard. But Lon took care of the town and Johnson handled county matters so they didn't tangle with each other.'

'Is there anything you can tell me that might help my investigation? I'm gonna talk to everyone around town so don't be afraid you'll be sticking your neck out. I won't mention names to anyone, whatever I learn. All I need is to be pointed in the right direction and I'll do the rest myself.'

'I'm real sorry, Marshal. I wish I could help.' Larter shook his head. 'There's nothing I can tell you.'

'The trouble around here will get worse if nobody stands up,' Carson said grimly.

'If you get some of the others to speak up then you can count me in, but not until.' Larter shook his head. 'I spend most of my time here alone, and I wouldn't stand a chance if I opened my mouth and someone got wind of it. They could get to me in here with no trouble, and no one would be any the wiser till next morning. No, sir, I know it ain't the right attitude, but the law ain't strong in these parts and I got to take care of myself.'

Carson nodded and turned on his heel. He kept to the shadows when he departed, then froze in the darkness when he caught the sound of approaching hooves. It sounded like several horses, and he moved slightly to gain better cover.

Moments later three riders materialised out of the darkness along the street and reined in before the entrance to the stable. Carson was standing only yards from them, his face averted from the light, his dark clothing blending with the shadows. As he studied the trio, shapeless figures in the night, one of them was not slow in giving orders in a harsh voice.

'Wiley, you and Raynor take a look around the street. Find that marshal and size him up. But don't start anything. I'm gonna check with the boss, and I'll see you in Norton's saloon in thirty minutes. You got that? No trouble.'

'OK, Mabry,' came the growled reply. 'We got it straight. There won't be no trouble.'

'They say this new marshal is faster and tougher than his brother,' the third man said harshly.

'That don't mean a thing.' One of the others chuckled.

Carson clenched his teeth as he listened. Two of the men dismounted and led their horses into the barn. The man called Mabry wheeled his horse and rode at a walk back along the street. Carson watched for a moment, wondering why Lon should have told Annie that he thought Mabry was responsible for robbing the bank in Prescott. He shook his head, his mind filled with questions, then set out on foot through the shadows, trailing Mabry, intent on learning what he had in mind. It looked like being a long, eventful night, Carson thought, but if he made any kind of progress then he would be satisfied.

FIVE

Mabry rode his horse at a walk along the street until he reached the law office, where he dismounted and tied his horse to the hitch-rail. Carson waited until the rancher had entered the office then moved to the window overlooking the street and peered inside, his eyes narrowing as he took in the scene.

Sheriff Rourke was seated behind his desk, his hat tipped forward over his eyes, his chair tilted backwards and his feet resting on the desk top. He scowled when his visitor slammed the street door, and pushed back his Stetson to glare at him.

'What in hell you making all that noise for, Mabry?' he demanded, his voice faintly audible to Carson's keen ears. 'And why are yuh in town in the middle of the week?'

'I heard Lon Carson's brother turned up and whipped Johnson with one hand tied behind his back.' Mabry chuckled. 'Wish I'd been here. It was time someone took that jughead down a peg or two. It don't do to throw weight around like Johnson did.'

'Yeah, he's been stompin' some at that. But he's finished now. The fool threw a slug at Matt

Carson, and him being a deputy U.S marshal, Johnson's gone in over his head this time.'

'I told you in the first place Johnson wasn't the kind of man you needed as a deputy. He's caused nothing but trouble since you pinned a badge on him.'

Carson frowned as he listened. He studied Mabry, seeing a tall, powerful man of about forty dressed in dirty range clothes. His heavy face was stubbled and he wore a bushy moustache. A cartridge belt was buckled around his waist, the holster tied down, and a bone-handled Colt nestled in the supple leather.

Carson shook his head. Mabry was a rancher but looked and acted like a gunhand, and here he was talking down to the sheriff. This situation needed checking out, especially because Lon had suspected Mabry of being concerned in the recent bank robbery. Sighing, Carson continued to listen, but the conversation in the office was general, touching on local affairs. And Rourke gave the impression that he did not like the way Mabry was talking to him, although he gave little indication of the fact beyond a harsh expression. Carson was relieved when Mabry turned suddenly and came to the door. He darted to the alley beside the jail and stepped into the darkness. Moments later Mabry passed by, leading his horse, and Carson slipped out of his concealment and followed at a discreet distance.

Mabry tethered his mount outside the saloon and entered the building, and when Carson peered in over the batwings he saw the rancher talking to his two men, who were both tough-looking, dressed in range clothes and armed. Ash Norton was behind the bar, and did not seem too interested in Mabry, for after serving the man the saloon owner moved to the other end of the bar and picked up a mail order catalogue, which he read with great concentration.

Carson pushed through the batwings and walked to the near corner of the bar, where Norton was lounging. The saloonman looked up at him, and an expression akin to relief fleetingly crossed his face.

'Howdy, Marshal,' he greeted. 'Yuh been taking a look-see around town, huh?'

'There ain't much to see.' Carson shook his head. He noted that Mabry was gazing at him with interest. 'I'd like to have a talk with you, in private.'

'Sure.' Norton frowned as he tried to read significance in Carson's expressionless face. 'Give me a couple of minutes. My tender will be back shortly. What'll you have to drink? It's on the house, remember?'

'A beer.' Carson leaned an elbow on the bar and looked around the saloon. There were at least two dozen men in the big room but no one was around Mabry and his two hardcases, he noted. He drank from the foaming glass of beer which Norton slid before him, and straightened casually when Mabry came towards him.

'Howdy,' greeted the rancher. 'I'm Cal Mabry, and I wanta tell you how sorry I am your brother was killed. He kept this town on the rails, and I sure hope you get the deadwood on the galoot who shot him.'

'Thanks,' Carson responded. 'My brother's death was a bad business, and I'll find his killer before I quit.'

'I wish you luck,' Mabry nodded. 'If there's anything I can do to help then let me know. You made a good start by taking Ham Johnson down a peg. It was on the cards he'd brace the wrong man before he was through.'

'Yeah.' Carson picked up his glass and drank deeply.

The bartender appeared at that moment and Ash Norton came along the bar, his keen gaze on Carson's face.

'We can have that talk now,' he said. 'In my office.'

Carson followed the saloonman into the office, and Norton heaved a sigh of relief as he closed the door.

'Cal Mabry is a hardcase,' he observed, indicating a chair beside his big desk.

'He'd need to be, operating a cattle spread in these parts,' Carson replied as he sat down.

'That ain't exactly what I mean and I think you know it.' Norton seated himself and leaned his elbows on the desktop. 'There's more to Mabry than shows. He came up from Texas five years ago, and I figure he was mixed up in some kind of trouble down that way.'

'What kind of trouble?'

Norton shook his head. 'You got me there. But I can sum up a man with the best of them, and there's something about Mabry I don't cotton to.'

'I don't deal in suspicion.' Carson shook his head. 'Give me some hard facts and I'll act on them.'

Norton nodded. He reached for a bottle of whisky and poured a generous measure into a glass. Looking at Carson, he motioned with the bottle and raised his eyebrows in silent invitation.

'No thanks.' Carson shook his head. 'Tell me, are you paying protection money?'

Norton's eyes narrowed, and for a moment he remained silent. Then he shrugged. 'You don't waste any time, Marshal. There are some in town who are paying money on the side for protection, but I ain't one of them. I own all the saloons in town and I have some tough men on my payroll.'

'Who's running the racket?'

Norton shook his head. 'No one is saying anything. It's a well kept secret. I'm on the town council, and we were discussing this matter only the other day. Needless to say, we didn't get very far with it.'

'You've talked it over with the sheriff?'

'Rourke is practically useless as a lawman.'

'Then why is he tolerated? You soon found a new town marshal when Lon was killed.'

Norton shook his head. 'I've been agitating for a shake-up in the law department, but I'm always out-voted. The man you need to talk to is Otto Kunkel. He's the town mayor.'

'You don't like Kunkel?'

'I never said that.'

'You don't have to.' Carson got to his feet. 'I'll talk to you again after I've been around a few days. When you learn that you can trust me you might open up a bit and tell me what's been going on around here.'

'A loose lip can get a man into a lot of trouble,'

Norton retorted.

Carson left the office and headed for the bat-wings. He noted that Mabry was no longer at the bar, although his two men were, and they subjected Carson to a close inspection as he passed. He went out to the street and turned in the direction of the store. The batwings creaked before he had covered many yards, and, glancing over his shoulder, he saw Mabry's men standing on the sidewalk. His right hand rested on the butt of his holstered gun as he continued along the sidewalk.

He reached the store, which was still open, and paused in the doorway to glance around the darkened street. The town seemed deserted, but the two men who had ridden in with Mabry were coming along the sidewalk.

Mabry's horse was now tethered in front of the store, and Carson entered the building and paused on the threshold. The place smelled of just about every commodity ever manufactured: leather, tobacco, fresh-ground coffee, dried and pickled fish, cheese, and the musty tang of new fabric in bolts. On the right a counter and shelves were piled with dry goods and hardware, and on the left was a counter for groceries. Not an inch of space was wasted. Cooking pots and slabs of bacon and hams were suspended from the rafters. And around the floor space were barrels and kegs brimming with sugar, flour, molasses and vinegar. There were canisters and boxes of spices and condiments, sacks of seasonal produce, and, on the counter, big glass jars of candy sticks and peppermint balls. A large, pot-bellied stove stood in the centre of the floor space.

Carson wrinkled his nose as he was assailed by the smells of the establishment. He saw Mabry entering a back room, accompanied by Otto Kunkel, and frowned, wanting to hear what passed between the two men. At the stable Mabry had said he wanted to check with his boss. Apparently that was not the sheriff, and now he was here to talk with Kunkel.

There was an assistant standing behind one of the counters, a tall, thin man in shirt sleeves, with sleeve protectors reaching to his elbows. He was watching Carson intently, and Carson moved towards him.

'Howdy,' Carson greeted. 'I wanta talk to Otto Kunkel.'

'Yes, sir. Otto is busy right now. Would you mind waiting a few minutes? I'll tell him you're here soon as he's free.'

Carson nodded and turned away to inspect the store in more detail, but his gaze missed nothing of his surroundings. He saw Mabry's two men standing on the sidewalk outside the doorway, and both were peering into the store. A woman appeared, pushing between the men, and brushed past Carson on her way to the counter. He went to the opposite counter and looked around, wishing he was in a position to hear what was passing between Mabry and the storekeeper.

'I'll see Kunkel later,' he called to the man at the counter, and turned on his heel and departed quickly. Outside he came up against Mabry's men, and they stepped aside as he reached them. He went on along the sidewalk, and when he glanced back over his shoulder he saw the men waiting stolidly outside the store. He stepped into a nearby alley and paused, realizing it was the one in which Lon was killed.

What had Lon been doing in the alley? Had he heard something suspicious on his last round of the day, or had he intended to eavesdrop on Kunkel for some reason? Carson shook his head and moved through the darkness towards a lighted window in the side wall of the store, aware that he was placing himself at a disadvantage by outlining himself against the light. But he needed to know what was passing between Mabry and Kunkel.

Reaching the window, he craned forward to peer inside, and saw Kunkel sitting at a desk with Mabry standing to one side. Mabry was talking and Kunkel was shaking his head, evidently disagreeing with what was being said. Carson suppressed a sigh. He could not hear a word. He glanced towards the street, expecting to see Mabry's men there watching him, but they were not in sight and he wondered what their duties were. He continued to watch the two men inside the office but could learn nothing from their attitudes or manner. Impatience filled him, and at that moment a gunshot hammered out the dense silence of the town and a string of raucous echoes fled through the dark night.

Carson started in shock but acted instinctively, turning towards the street and running with long strides. He hit the sidewalk and paused, ears keened to locate the direction from which the shot had sounded. Dull echoes were growling menacingly from along the street in the direction of the law office, and he stepped into the street and ran fast towards the jail.

Mabry's two men were standing stolidly in front of the store, and Carson glanced at them in passing. They remained motionless, watching him, and Carson crossed the street and continued to the law office. Men were emerging from Norton's saloon as he passed, their voices demanding information about the shot.

Carson reached the law office and thrust open the door. The office was deserted, but the door in the back wall leading into the cell block was ajar and he crossed to it and entered the narrow passage between two rows of cells. Sheriff Rourke was standing in a locked cell, leaning heavily against the barred door. There was blood on Rourke's shirt front and the lawman's craggy face was ashen with shock. Carson went to the cell. A faint trace of gunsmoke was hanging in the air, and he wrinkled his nose at its pungency.

'What happened?' Carson was breathing hard from his run.

Rourke groaned. 'Johnson banged on his cell door, and when I came to check with him he sneaked my gun from its holster and took my keys. He locked me in here, and shot me before he left.'

Carson grasped the door of the cell and tried to open it. He suppressed a sigh when he found it locked.

'Where's the key?' he demanded.

'I guess Johnson took it with him. There's a spare bunch in the right-hand drawer of my desk.'

Carson fetched the keys and unlocked the door.

He checked the sheriff's wound, saw that it was superficial, and began to relax.

'You're not badly hurt,' he observed. 'Why would Johnson risk shooting if he didn't mean to kill you? He must have known a shot would rouse the town.'

'I'm gonna see Doc Hayman.' Rourke left the cell block and went into the office. The street door was open and half a dozen townsmen stood on the threshold. They began asking questions, and the sheriff pushed his way through them and departed.

Carson paused in the office, listening to the questions of the townsmen. The street door was opened and Shap Newman entered. The town marshal was holding his sixgun in his hand.

'I heard a shot,' Newman rapped. 'What happened?'

Carson explained, noting Newman's callous reaction to the grim news. The town marshal holstered his gun.

'I'll take a look around and see if I can find Johnson,' he said. 'He won't get far without a horse. I figure to catch him at the stable.'

He left the office and Carson followed, walking back along the street to Kunkel's store, his thoughts sluggish. The sheriff had deliberately turned Johnson loose, Carson was certain. The sheriff's wound was minor, and had probably been done to throw suspicion away from Rourke. That seemed fairly obvious. Johnson had put himself out on a limb by ambushing a deputy U.S. marshal and someone feared that he would reveal the true situation existing in town if he came to trial, so he had been freed.

Carson made his way to the hotel, ready to turn in. Tomorrow would be soon enough to pursue his enquiries. So far he had learned little but he had made progress and there were pointers to be followed. A good night's sleep would give his subconscious mind time in which to sift through what he had learned, and in the morning he would be ready to start applying pressure to certain members of the town community.

SIX

Joel was sitting in the lobby of the hotel when Carson entered, and the boy uttered an ejaculation of relief as he sprang up and ran to Carson's side.

'What's wrong?' demanded Carson.

'Ma thought of something she figgers you oughta know about before morning,' the youngster said tensely. 'Will you come to the shack now?'

'Sure.' Carson frowned as they left the hotel, for Joel seemed over-anxious.

Joel hurried to the alley that led to the back lots where the family shack was situated, and Carson reached out a hand and grasped the boy's shoulder.

'What's your hurry?' he asked. 'Stop right there, Joel. Something's bugging you and I wanta know what it is.'

The boy halted in the alley mouth, his face just a pale blur as he looked up at Carson.

'Ma said for me to hurry,' he replied, 'and I waited at the hotel a long time.'

Carson sensed the boy's uneasiness and shook his head. 'I figure you're lying, Joel,' he said.

'What's going on?'

For a few moments the boy remained silent, breathing heavily, then blurted out: 'It's Ham Johnson, Matt. He came to the shack and he's holding a gun on ma. He said for me to tell you to come quickly, and he means to get the drop on you when you walk into the shack.'

Carson clenched his hands. 'OK, Joel,' he said softly. 'Go back to the shack. Tell Johnson you gave me the message and I said I'll be along in a couple minutes – I'm busy right now because the sheriff was shot. You got that?'

'Sure, but Johnson is a mean galoot and he'd hurt ma if you call the wrong shot.'

'Don't worry about that. Get moving now, and when you're in the shack stick real close to your ma, huh?'

'Sure thing, Matt.' Relief sounded in the boy's thin tone. He ran off along the alley and quickly disappeared into the gloom.

Carson followed swiftly, moving silently, and he was right behind Joel when the boy reached the shack. Lanternlight was spilling from the window and Carson moved to it as Joel entered. A rough curtain partially covered the window but was ill-fitting, and Carson could see the interior of the crude building.

Annie was sitting on the edge of the bed in the far corner.

Ham Johnson was standing by the plank table opposite the window. At that moment Joel stepped into Carson's view, his voice barely audible as he told Johnson what Carson had said. Johnson scowled at the news and slapped Joel's face. The boy staggered and lost his balance, and Carson moved swiftly as Johnson bent and seized hold of Joel's shoulder. Reaching the door, Carson hit it with his left shoulder and sent it crashing open. He lunged into the room, right hand reaching for his holstered gun. Johnson was in the act of dragging Joel upright, and half turned towards the door as Carson crossed the threshold. He moved with surprising speed despite his shock, thrusting Joel away from him and reaching for the gun in his waistband.

Carson was upon him in two swift strides, and Johnson cursed when the hammer of his gun snagged in the rough material of his shirt. The weapon remained in his waistband, and, before he could extricate it, Carson hit him on the jaw with a sledging left hook, following up as Johnson went backwards on his heels across the shack, still trying to jerk his gun from his waistband.

'You wanta see me!' Carson spoke through clenched teeth. His left hand closed on Johnson's right wrist, and there was the sound of ripping cloth as he exerted pressure and forced Johnson's gun hand up shoulder high. The gun cleared Johnson's waistband, its muzzle pointing upwards as Carson twisted the man's wrist. Then Carson struck with his right fist, driving his hard knuckles into Johnson's belly with the force of a kicking mule.

Johnson's breath whooshed out of his gaping mouth, and Carson swung his right upwards to connect with the man's jaw. Johnson fell to the ground like a poleaxed steer, and Carson wrenched the gun out of his hand and stepped back, cocking the weapon and covering Johnson. But it was not needed. Blood was dribbling down Johnson's already battered features and he was unconscious, breathing stertorously through his slack mouth.

Joel had run to his mother's side and Annie was holding the boy. Their faces were etched with fear, and Carson sighed as he straightened.

'I'm getting a mite angry with the way Johnson is acting,' he said thinly. 'Did he harm you, Annie?'

'No, Matt,' she gasped. 'It was you he wanted.'

'Well he's got me now, and with the sheriff off duty with a bullet wound I'll put a stop to Johnson once and for all.'

He grasped Johnson's thick shoulder, shaking him roughly. Johnson groaned. His head lolled and his eyes flickered.

'OK, big man!' Carson's voice was harsh. 'You've sure made a heap of trouble for yourself. Get up and we'll go back to the jail, and this time you'll stay there.'

Under the menace of Carson's gun, Johnson got to his feet and lumbered unsteadily to the door. Carson followed closely.

'I'll be back to see you when I've settled this, Annie,' he said. 'Do what you can about fixing the door, huh?'

Johnson blundered through the alley, and Carson kept him under the muzzle of the gun in his hand. They reached the street and headed for the jail. A figure appeared suddenly on the sidewalk ahead of them, and Shap Newman's voice called a challenge that was filled with menace.

'Johnson, I got you dead to rights. Hold it right

there and throw up your hands.'

'You're too late, Newman,' Carson rapped, aware that the town marshal could not see him behind Johnson. 'I already got him, and this time he'll stay in jail.'

Newman came to Carson's side, gun in hand. 'You sure don't waste any time,' he said grudgingly. 'Where did you come across him? I been searching the town. I figured he would head for the stable, but he didn't go near the place.'

Carson did not answer. Johnson kept moving towards the jail, and when they entered the law office Carson was surprised to see Sheriff Rourke slumped in his chair at the desk.

'I didn't expect to see you again so soon,' Carson said.

'I wanta get my hands on Johnson,' the sheriff replied. 'So you picked him up again!'

'Yeah, and this time he's gonna stay behind bars.'

Newman picked up the jail keys from the desk. 'On your way, Johnson,' he rapped. 'You know where the cells are.'

'You think I turned Johnson loose?' the sheriff demanded, and Carson smiled, his eyes glinting.

'If I thought that, Rourke, you'd be in the cells right now, along with Johnson,' he responded. 'But I'll tell you this. I don't like the way the law here is being handled. You better start shaping up like a real lawman or there'll be some changes.'

'It ain't my fault,' Rourke blustered. 'You can see the kind of men I have to work with.'

'That's the point,' retorted Carson. 'I'm questioning the decision you made to take Johnson on in the first place. From what I've heard about him he's just a bullying hardcase.'

'He was the best available.' Rourke's face was pale, his eyes dull.

'Well we've put that right now.' Carson held out his hand for the jail keys when Newman returned to the office. 'I'll hold on to these while Johnson is inside,' he said firmly, and Newman handed them over without comment. 'You better go off duty now, Rourke,' he continued. 'Do you have a night jailer?'

'Not while I'm in town. I hit the sack in one of the cells.' Rourke was sullen.

Carson nodded. 'As of now, don't go near Johnson unless you're unarmed. I don't wanta lose him again. You got that?'

Rourke nodded and stood up. He lumbered towards the street door. 'I'll get me a drink before turning in,' he said. 'I need something to kill the pain. I got a key to get in here if you need to leave,' he added.

Newman followed Rourke to the door and they departed together. Carson paced the office, his thoughts harsh. He unlocked the door leading into the cell block and walked to the door of Johnson's cell. The big man was lying on the bunk against the far wall, his eyes closed against the dim light issuing from the single lantern. He squinted at Carson, recognised him and closed his eyes again.

'If you wanta save yourself a load of trouble you better come clean with me.' Carson's harsh tone rasped in the silence. 'You may not think so at the moment, but I'm probably the best friend you've got. All you have to do is tell me what's been going on around here and why my brother was killed and you can ride out legally. I'll turn you loose, and you got my word on that.'

'There ain't nothing I can tell you.' Johnson spoke with difficulty. His mouth was bruised, his lips swollen, and there was dried blood on his battered face.

Carson felt no pity for the man, and turned away when he realised that Johnson was not going to talk, but he paused by the connecting door and turned once more, to see Johnson sitting up and staring after him.

'Do you mean what you say? You'll turn me loose if I talk?' Johnson demanded.

'You got it.' Carson remained where he was. 'But the offer folds when I leave so you better make up your mind pronto. If you want a deal then start talking now.'

Johnson shook his head and settled down on the bunk again. He closed his eyes. 'There ain't a thing you can do about this,' he growled. 'Come tomorrow I'll be out of here permanent and you'll be heading for Boot Hill.'

Carson departed and locked the connecting door. So that was the way of it. Something bad was going on, and Johnson's attitude proved it. But Carson had no intention of letting the initiative slip away from him. He left the office, locking the door behind him, and set off along the street to the saloon. If things did not happen then it was time he did some pushing. Although he did not have much to go on there were a few loose ends which he had noted, and a little judicial string-pulling here and there might produce a favourable result.

The saloon was quiet, with a dozen men inside, although Carson noted that Mabry's two men, Wiley and Raynor, were playing cards at a corner table. Carson frowned when he did not see Sheriff Rourke present, for the lawman had left the office with the intention of getting a drink before turning in. And where was Shap Newman? It was unlikely that the town marshal was making yet another round of the apparently quiet town.

Ash Norton was not behind the bar. The tender looked up from reading a magazine, and came forward immediately, smiling.

'Ash said everything you want is on the house,' he said.

'Beer, and I'll pay for it,' Carson responded. He smiled. 'I wouldn't want folks around here getting the wrong idea. They might think I was accepting a bribe.'

'Not the brother of Lon Carson!' The tender produced a tall glass of beer and Carson slapped a silver coin on the bar.

'It seems everyone liked my brother,' he mused.

The bartender nodded. 'He was a good lawman.'

'Then why won't anyone speak up about what happened to him?' Carson's voice had taken on an edge, and the tender met his hard gaze and then looked away. 'Someone in town must know. I already been told there were no strangers around, so a townsman must have pulled the trigger on Lon. That's how much the folks here thought of him, huh? He was killed protecting lives and property and no one is willing to speak up.'

The tender shook his head. 'I don't figger it like

that. It was just like I say. No one knows what happened.'

'It won't be a mystery much longer.' Carson drank his beer, picked up his change and left.

The big store was being closed when Carson looked in at the doorway. Otto Kunkel was counting money at the counter. He looked up quickly at the sound of Carson's boots rapping on the pine floor and a gun appeared in his right hand, levelling quickly at Carson. Kunkel's eyes narrowed as he cocked the Colt.

'You expecting trouble?' demanded Carson.

'I didn't recognize you immediately.' Kunkel uncocked the gun and laid it aside. 'I don't expect trouble but I'm ready for it. I heard you wanted to talk to me. I'm sorry I was busy when you called.'

'Most of the town businessmen are paying protection money.' Carson spoke bluntly, hoping to shock Kunkel into an admission. But the big storekeeper merely shook his head.

'I don't know about that,' he said. 'I wouldn't pay it.' His pale eyes narrowed as he regarded Carson's inscrutable face. 'You have proof of this thing? Has someone told you about it?'

'How else would I know?' Carson countered. 'So you're not paying, huh?'

'No. I do not pay anyone.'

'So what makes you different from everybody else? In a case like this there are no exceptions. And who did you say no to? I don't believe no one approached you. From what I've seen of this burg, you're the biggest fish in Cattle Creek.'

'Mebbe I am too big to mess with.' Kunkel pushed back his shoulders. 'I got fingers in several pies around here. I own half a share in the livery and I got an interest in a local cattle ranch. If anyone tried to put the bite on me I could soon have a dozen tough cowhands in here looking out for my interests.'

Carson narrowed his eyes as he digested the information. 'So that was why Cal Mabry came in to talk to you,' he mused. 'You got an interest in his cowspread.'

'Is that against the law?' Kunkel's pale eyes glittered.

'My brother was killed in the alley beside this store.'

'You figure that because he was killed on my doorstep I should know who did it?'

'Nope. I'm merely gonna ask if you saw or heard anything suspicious on the night it happened.'

Kunkel shook his head. His fleshy face was set in harsh lines. 'I wish I could tell you something that might help you find the killer.'

Carson turned away, then paused and faced the storekeeper again. 'If you do remember anything then look me up, huh?'

'Sure. I'd do that without being asked.' Kunkel returned to counting his money, and Carson went out to the sidewalk, feeling that no matter which way he turned, he was fenced in, and until he broke through the wall of silence he would learn nothing about the events leading up to his brother's death.

He went on to Annie's shack. She had a pistol in her hand when she opened the door to him. Joel was lying in a made-up bed by the fireplace, but he was not asleep, and sat up quickly when Carson entered.

'Did Johnson give you any trouble?' demanded the boy.

Carson shook his head. 'He ain't big enough to do that, and you know it,' he said.

'But there are some around here who are big enough to give you problems,' cut in Annie. 'You'd best be careful, Matt.'

'Have you thought of anything that might help me?' queried Carson. 'I've been asking questions around but nobody is keen to talk. I ask myself if they're all as scared as they seem.'

'They have reason to be scared.' Annie shook her head. 'They know Lon was murdered because he discovered something, and they realised the same thing will happen to them if they talk.'

'Tell me about Otto Kunkel. He interests me. He's making big tracks around here, huh?'

'He's steadily expanding his business interests. But that's not against the law. And he's a kind man, Matt. Anyone needing a hand-out has only to ask Otto. He gives credit in his store, and doesn't press for payment if someone falls on hard times.'

'He told me he owns half the livery stable, and he's got an interest in a local ranch. That would be Cal Mabry's place?'

'That's right. Mabry was hit by rustlers last year, and would have gone under if Otto hadn't bailed him out.'

Carson stifled a yawn. 'I guess I'm trying too hard,' he mused. 'Right now nothing is making sense. I figure to turn in and forget everything until tomorrow. Goodnight, Annie. I'll see you around, and keep thinking about Lon's business. I need all the help I can get if I'm to beat this thing.'

'Sure.' Annie smiled wanly.

Carson took his leave and walked through the darkness of the back lots, making for the main street. He had to check out the law office again before he could consider himself finished for the day, and his thoughts centred on the sheriff. Where had Rourke gone when he left the office? And Newman had slipped out of sight. What a poor picture of lawmen that pair made, he mused. The sheriff was apparently long past his usefulness, and Newman looked like he shouldn't be trusted an inch.

He walked along the shadowed street, staying off the boardwalk, preferring silent movement in the dust. A piano was playing in the building where Carson had seen several girls on the balcony earlier, and he nodded to himself. That was probably where Newman was right now. But he was more interested in the sheriff at that moment and continued to the law office.

Rourke was in the office, sitting at the desk and looking exhausted. His face was pale. There was a bloodstained bandage on his upper right arm. He scowled and shook his head.

'I'm getting too old for this job,' he said.

'Yeah, that's what it looks like,' Carson agreed. 'And the remedy is simple.'

'You don't like me, huh?' Rourke smiled sadly.

Carson shook his head. 'I don't know you well enough to form an opinion. What I don't like is the way you're letting law work slide around here. If you can't do the job properly then get out. It's as simple as that.'

'It ain't simple at all.' Rourke shook his head. 'I

can't quit until I know what happened to your brother.'

'Lon's been dead three weeks and you ain't learned a thing in that time. What makes you think you'll be any luckier now I've showed up?'

'You're the kind of man who makes things happen. I was like that myself when I was younger. Look what's happened since you arrived today. You've put Johnson where he belongs, and half the businessmen in town are running scared because you're stirring up the water. I know there's bad things going on around here, but I can't put a finger on who's responsible. I'm gonna have to leave that to you, but I'm ready to back you up when you make your play, and I want you to know that.'

'OK!' Carson nodded, wondering why the sheriff was changing his attitude. 'We'll talk some more about this tomorrow. Right now I'm more than ready to hit the sack. It's getting so I can't think straight. You're bedding down in the cells, huh? So stay out of Johnson's reach. I wanta find him behind bars come morning.'

'He'll still be here,' Rourke nodded. 'And so will all the problems you've got.'

Carson was certain of that, and when he departed he thought over the sheriff's words. If he was making progress it sure didn't feel like it. He made his way along the street to the hotel, and as he stepped on to the sidewalk in front of it a shadow moved in an adjacent alley. He reacted instinctively, reaching for his gun and throwing himself down into the dust, his muscles tensed for the slamming impact of a bullet fired from cover.

He cocked his sixgun and pushed back the brim of his Stetson.

But nothing happened. The shadow had faded back into the darkness of the alley. Carson frowned as his tension eased.

'Who's there?' he called, his voice echoing in the silence. 'Show yourself. It's dangerous to sneak around in the dark.'

'Are you Lon Carson's brother?' The question hissed through the darkness.

'Yeah, I'm Matt Carson. Who are you and what do you want? You are playing a dangerous game, stalking me. I've caught sight of you twice already this evening.'

'I need to talk to you and I don't want to be seen. You are a lawman, aren't you?'

'I am.' Carson was trying to decide whether the voice was male or female and if it was trying to lure him into a trap. 'What's your problem?'

'Can we talk?'

'Sure thing.' Carson eased forward the hammer of his gun, uncocking the big weapon, but he did not move, still suspecting a trap.

'I can't risk being seen talking to you.' It was a woman's voice, Carson decided.

'Come on out into the open where I can see you and then we'll decide what to do,' he responded.

His keen eyes caught a glimpse of movement in the darkness of the alley and then a slight figure appeared from the deceptive shadows. It was a woman, but Carson did not take any chances. He pushed himself to one knee, ears strained for suspicious sounds, his gun still in his hand.

'Please come into the alley.' The woman's voice

was tense, vibrant with fear, and Carson released his pent up breath in a long sigh. This was where he had to start taking risks.

SEVEN

Carson moved towards the alley, alert for trickery, keeping the woman between himself and the denser shadows. He expected gunfire to erupt from the surrounding darkness but reached her side without incident and flattened himself against a wall.

'What's your problem?' he demanded, recalling the figure he had seen before lurking in the background. 'I figure you've been dogging me since I hit town. I was shot at earlier, and you're lucky I didn't peg you for the ambusher.'

'It was Ham Johnson shooting at you,' came the surprising reply.

'How'd you know that?'

'I saw him. I've been trying to get to you ever since you rode into town. I saw you from the balcony of the dance hall opposite the law office, and one of the other girls said you were Lon Carson's brother, a State lawman come to right the wrongs around here.'

'I'm not here on federal business. But I am gonna find the man who killed Lon although I haven't struck gold yet with my questions around town. Folks are scared to talk.'

'I'm not. I'm too desperate. Look, I'm supposed to be sick in my room at the dance hall, and if they check up on me and find me missing then my life won't be worth a plugged nickel.'

'OK. Tell me what you want to say and then head on back before they miss you.' Carson holstered his gun and brushed dust from his clothes. 'You can talk to me on the move. What's on your mind? I figure you've got to be in real bad trouble to go to these lengths to get to me.'

'You're a hard man to get to. You're being watched closely, and I'm surprised they ain't killed you already.'

Carson moistened his lips. He knew his life was always on the line, but it was chilling to hear the fact stated so bluntly. He recalled Mabry's words to his two men, Wiley and Raynor, and knew the girl was speaking the truth.

'They may want to kill me,' he observed, 'but it wouldn't look so good if I was shot three weeks after my brother died. But let's get down to business. What's your name?'

'I'm Dora Hand. Ham Johnson figgers I'm his girl, and he's giving me trouble to make me toe the line.'

'Is that so? Well your trouble is over. Johnson is in jail, and he won't be out for years.'

'You'll never keep him in jail. I saw him walk out after you locked him up, and although you caught him again he won't be behind bars long.'

'Start at the beginning,' Carson suggested. He glanced around the street. They were in deep shadow, but people were on the sidewalks, and the batwings of Norton's big saloon were in almost perpetual motion.

'Ham Johnson is an outlaw from Texas, part of a gang that moved up this way because it got too hot for them down south.'

'Give me names,' Carson said, 'and by morning the whole bunch will be behind bars.'

'It's not as easy as that.' She sounded hesitant. 'My pa is mixed up with them. He was on the wrong side of the law in Texas until I got him away from all that. We came this way to make a fresh start, and Pa was doing all right until Johnson and the others showed up. Johnson made Pa go back to brand blotting, and he's holding that over me to make me stick around Cattle Creek, playing me and pa one against the other.'

'I've heard there's rustling on the range. Did you approach my brother about this?'

'I did, in the week before he was killed, but I only hinted at it because I was afraid my pa would get dragged in with the others.'

'So that was why Lon is dead! He began to check up on your information and they killed him!'

'It looks like that.' Her voice tremored as she spoke. 'I wish now I'd kept quiet, but something's got to be done about these outlaws.'

'You're right,' Carson nodded. 'And all you've got to do is put names to the outlaws and I'll handle the rest of it.'

'What about my pa?'

'I can't make any promises. If he's mixed up in the rustling and nothing else then I might be able to do something for him. But my brother has been killed, and there was a bank robbery in Prescott in which a man was killed. Those crimes are serious and someone will hang for them.'

'Pa wasn't in on that. Cal Mabry handled the bank robbery. That was his line of business in Texas. The Rangers were after him down south so he headed for these parts and brought his gang with him. In Texas he called himself Pete Yago. Check with the Texas Rangers and they'll tell you all about him.'

'Where is your pa?' Carson's mind was buzzing with the information, but he was cautious enough to be aware that she might be lying, hoping to lead him into a trap, although her words had a ring of truth about them.

'He's at a line shack on Mabry's range. They're stealing cattle from all over the range and Pa is blotting brands with a running iron. He's real good at it, an artist. You'd need to kill a steer to check whether its brand has been altered if Pa did it.'

'Does your pa wanta quit?'

'He sure does. But Johnson is blackmailing him, using me as the lever, and he's keeping me quiet here in town by threatening to kill Pa if I don't toe the line. Johnson takes me out to the shack every month or so to see Pa, and from what Pa says, I figger he wants to break away.'

'How many rustlers are at the shack?'

'Usually half a dozen. Tough men who were in Mabry's gang down in Texas.'

'How far is the shack from here?'

'About three hours in the saddle.'

'Are you willing to show me the way?'

'Now?' Surprise edged her voice.

'Sure. I like to strike while the iron is hot.'

Carson's tone was harsh. 'Listen. If I get the deadwood on those rustlers come the dawn then you and your pa can quit this neck of the woods with no questions asked. Is that a deal?'

'So long as you can keep Ham Johnson away from me.'

'Then it's a deal.' Carson glanced around. 'Can you ride in those clothes you're wearing?'

'Sure. I'm ready to go right now. What about horses?'

'Mine's at the stable. We can get one there for you.'

She accompanied him through the shadows and he stopped off at the hotel to collect his saddlebags and rifle. He paused at the reception desk to speak to the bored-looking clerk.

'I'm real tired,' he said. 'I was on the trail more than a week before I got here, and I'm gonna hit the sack now and catch up on pounding my ear. I don't wanta be disturbed, no matter who comes calling. You got that?'

'Anything you say.' The clerk handed over the room key.

'Thanks.' Carson ascended the stairs, let himself into the room, and locked himself in. He gathered his saddlebags and rifle and used the window to get out on the balcony overlooking the street. There was a flight of wooden steps at one end of the balcony that led down into an alley beside the hotel, and Carson descended silently.

Dora was waiting for him in the shadows and they continued to the stable. He warned her to remain out of sight while he fetched horses, his mind buzzing with the information she had given him, and the actions of some of the men he had already met in town now seemed to make sense.

He entered the stable, saddled up his black, then went to dicker with the stableman to rent a horse for Dora. Larter was in his office, and Carson impressed the need for secrecy on the man when they came to terms over a horse.

'I'm a law abiding man,' Larter said. 'I'll do anything you say. I don't know who's gonna ride out of town with you, and, if anyone asks, I won't know where you're going, which I don't.'

'If Annie Carson comes asking, you can tell her I'm OK and will be back soon. Would you do that?'

'Sure thing, and good luck.' Larter saddled a horse and Carson departed, swinging into the saddle of the black and leading the rented horse.

Dora emerged from the nearby shadows and mounted swiftly. Carson glanced around as they faded back into the night and left Cattle Creek, hoping that their departure was undetected. Once clear of the town, Dora changed direction until they were riding west, and when they hit a well-defined trail they continued at a canter through the starry night.

Carson was thoughtful on the long ride. They talked little, and he remained alert, not wanting to be surprised on the trail. The moon appeared, shedding soft yellow light over the range, and a keen breeze blew into their faces as they rode.

Eventually Dora reined up and slid wearily out of the saddle. Carson dismounted at her side.

'This is as close as we can ride without warning them we're here,' she said. 'These outlaws are like hunting dogs. Most of them sleep with one eye open.'

'I know the breed,' Carson replied. 'We'll leave the horses hereabouts.' He glanced at the sky, which was lightening towards the east. 'There's still an hour or so to dawn. You can turn in on my blankets while I take a look around.'

'I'm too excited to sleep,' she said. 'And I better point out the shack to you. It's by a creek just over the rise there.'

'You settle down and stay put,' he insisted. 'I'll mosey around and pick up the details for myself. When it's light enough for me to see what I'm doing I'll make my play. If you hear shooting, don't let it throw you. Stay out of sight here and I'll come back to you.'

'Don't you consider that you might be killed?'

'Nope. It don't come into my calculations.' He untied his blanket roll. 'Hit the sack. I'll be back later.'

He departed silently, making for the rise she had indicated. Bellying forward on the ridge, he found himself looking down on a creek shimmering in the moonlight. There was a shack nearby on a knoll, and a pole corral to one side holding eight horses. Carson studied the area intently, looking for the presence of a guard, and soon spotted the faint red glow of a cigarette. He made out the shape of a man hunched in the shelter of an oak tree.

So they had a guard out, which proved to him the kind of men they were. He remained motionless, watching the guard, working on his plan of action, but within a few moments the guard got to his feet and went into the shack. Yellow lamplight flared at an unglazed window, and Carson heard the guard calling to the sleeping men inside.

During the next few minutes the occupants of the shack arose and went about their morning chores. It looked to Carson that they were preparing to ride out, and he eased back over the ridge and went to where Dora was lying on his blankets. When he acquainted her with the news she got to her feet.

'They'll be going to rustle stock,' she said. 'Can I get to my pa? If I can I talk to him I might be able to stop him riding with them.'

Carson nodded. He had been thinking along the same lines. 'Come with me,' he said. 'I need you to point out your pa anyway. I figure to play this as it comes.'

She followed him as he sneaked back over the ridge, and they worked their way down towards the corral. Smoke was rising from the tall chimney of the shack. The rustlers were having breakfast. Dawn was approaching, the sky lightening perceptibly towards the east, and details of the surrounding area were slowly becoming clearer.

Carson hunkered down in cover between the corral and the shack and pulled Dora down beside him. He warned her to remain motionless and silent, and they waited out the minutes while the rustlers ate breakfast. Then three men emerged from the shack and came towards the corral, passing within feet of Carson's position. They began saddling horses.

Moments passed and three other men emerged from the shack and began to saddle up. Carson looked at Dora and raised an eyebrow, asking a silent question, and the girl shook her head. Her father was still in the shack. She put her mouth to Carson's ear.

'Pa does the cooking here. He's cleaning pans, I guess.'

The six men were soon ready to ride, and they swung into their saddles. One came to the door of the shack and reined in.

'Joe, it's time we hit the trail,' he called. 'You're always last.'

A tall, thin man emerged from the shack and stood blinking in the early morning light. He was in his fifties, Carson guessed, and his bearded face was gaunt.

'That's my pa,' Dora hissed in Carson's ear.

'Why am I always last?' Joe Hand demanded irritably. 'You fellers eat the grub I cook and then you're ready to ride, but I got to clean up and pack the grub you'll eat on on the range before I'm ready to go.'

'We'll be riding,' the mounted man cut in. 'You'll have to catch up. You know where we're heading.'

'Sure. I'll be along when I'm ready.'

Carson sighed with relief when the riders departed at a fast clip. They headed north and soon disappeared around the creek. There were two horses remaining in the corral, and Carson guessed that one of them was a pack horse.

'Let me talk to my pa,' Dora said.

'Call him,' Carson advised. 'I want him out in the open.'

Dora gazed at him, uncertainty showing in her pale eyes. 'You wouldn't go back on your word now you're here, would you?' she demanded.

'Nope. But there might be another man in that shack with your pa, and I can handle him better out here.'

She nodded and called her father's name. He emerged from the shack, peering around, and Dora arose and emerged from cover,

'Pa, are you alone now?' she demanded.

'Dora! What in tarnation are you doin' here?' He glanced around suspiciously. 'Where's Johnson?'

'Are you alone now, Pa?'

'Sure. But how'd you get here?'

Carson arose, palming his Colt as he did so for Joe Hand was wearing a pistol on his right hip.

'I brought her,' he said. 'Just stand still and don't do anything with your hands.'

'What's going on?' Joe Hand frowned. 'What game are you playing, Dora?'

'Let's go into the shack,' Carson suggested. 'Take out your gun and drop it, Joe.'

The rustler obeyed, his expression stony. Carson scooped up the discarded weapon and followed as Dora entered the shack with her father, and he remained silent while she acquainted him with the situation. Joe Hand listened in silence, his pale gaze on Carson, and distrust showed plainly in his eyes.

'I don't like it,' he said finally. 'You shouldn't have done it, Dora. There's no way out of this.'

'What's been stopping you from quitting?' Carson asked. 'If Dora is to be believed, you're with this gang because you and she can't get away together.'

'That's right. Johnson has been calling the

shots. He threatened to kill Dora if I didn't toe the line.'

'Well she ain't in town now,' Carson observed. 'And the two of you are free to ride in any direction you want.'

'What's the catch?' Joe Hand was not convinced.

'There's no catch.' Carson shook his head. 'I made a deal with Dora and she's kept her side of it. She gave me information and led me here, so you're both free to ride out.'

'And Ham Johnson is in jail?' Hand demanded.

'He sure is,' Dora said gleefully, 'and the marshal here gave him the beating of his life before putting a slug through his arm. You're wasting time, Pa. Let's get out of here.'

'There's one thing I'll ask you to do before you quit this range,' Carson said. 'I want to catch this gang red-handed, hazing stolen stock. Show me where they're heading before you pull out.'

'You got a deal,' Hand said. He was shaking his head as if the developments were too much to take in. 'But you don't figure to handle that bunch alone, huh?'

'That's my problem, and you can leave me to worry about it,' Carson replied.

'They're gonna hit Hesp's Bar H. They'll bring the herd back to Mabry's range. I'm supposed to meet them at Oak Ridge and blot the brands before the cows reach here. I'll saddle up and take you to Oak Ridge. It's about five miles from here, and by the time I reach it the gang will have the cattle on the move from Hesp's range.'

Carson nodded and Joe Hand went to the corral and saddled up. They set out for Oak Ridge, and as they hit rising ground, Carson dropped behind to ride at Dora's side. Joe Hand, leading the way, suddenly uttered a warning cry, and Carson looked ahead and saw a rider coming towards them. He recognised the man as one of the six who had ridden out from the shack.

The rider was quickly upon them, and reined in, reaching for his holstered gun when he saw Carson.

'What's going on?' he demanded. 'Who's this, Joe?'

Carson put a hand to his gun, and palmed it when he saw the man intended drawing his weapon. The man was slow, but he continued his movement despite being covered by Carson's gun.

'Drop it,' Carson snapped. He waited until the last possible moment, and, when the newcomer continued to draw, he fired a shot, aiming for the man's shoulder.

Their horses started at the crash of the shot and the rustler jerked, then pitched out of his saddle. Carson gigged his horse forward, still covering the man, and dismounted. The rustler had dropped his gun and lay groaning, a splotch of blood on his right shoulder. Carson kicked the fallen gun clear and bent to check the man, removing a knife from his belt.

'It's Hank Wenn,' Joe Hand said, coming to Carson's side. 'He rode out with the others. I wonder why he turned back?'

Carson examined the man's wound. The bullet had struck the collar bone, shattering it, and blood was seeping fast. He staunched the wound, using the man's dusty neckerchief.

'I'll ride on alone from here,' Carson decided. 'I can follow tracks. You're free to ride where you want.'

'What about Wenn?' Dora asked. 'You can't leave him.'

'He won't want to go far with that wound. Take him back to the shack and leave him there. I'll collect him when I've settled with the other rustlers.'

He swung into his saddle and turned away, intent upon his duty. When he glanced back over his shoulder he saw Dora and Joe Hand escorting the wounded man back the way they had come, and he faced his front and rode fast, following tracks that were plain in the dust.

By mid-morning Carson was on high ground, and just ahead were the five riders he had been following for hours. A large herd of cattle was grazing in the distance, and when the riders began to fan out to surround the herd, Carson knew that at last he was in business.

Keeping in cover, he waited until the herd was on the move then eased forward into a position from which he could shoot at an angle. He emptied his Winchester over the heads of the leaders, stampeding the herd and sending it back across the range. The sudden shooting shocked the rustlers but they came towards him instantly, firing rapidly, and Carson transferred his aim to them, shooting mercilessly, knocking one of them out of his saddle before they were aware of what was going on.

The others kept coming forward, and bullets snarled around Carson. He ducked and kept shooting, breathing acrid gunsmoke as a fight developed. The rustlers began to close in around him like predators scenting a kill, and Carson was grimly content to take them on.

EIGHT

A bullet clipped the crown of Carson's hat, and, as he changed position another punched through the top of his left shoulder. He dropped his rifle and lay full length behind his cover, ears filled with the heavy racket of shooting. Clenching his teeth against the pain in his shoulder he drew his sixgun. Two of the rustlers were working their way around to cut him off from his horse. He rolled to the left then eased up once more and looked for a target. A rustler was running through the brush to the left, and Carson swung his Colt and fired. The man went down with threshing limbs.

Carson grabbed his rifle and changed position. Sweat was beading his forehead. The sun was hot overhead. He eased back towards his horse, which was standing in deep cover. Gun echoes were fading, and then silence came. He lay motionless, watching for movement, aware that the rustlers would not leave. They needed to put him out of action before they could quit or make another try for the herd.

He heard brush crackle nearby under a furtive foot and cocked his sixgun. Pain was stabbing through the wound in his shoulder and he could feel blood dribbling down his arm. He removed his neckerchief, shook the dust from it, then padded it and thrust it inside his shirt against the wound. Feet suddenly pounded and two men appeared, running towards him, firing as they came.

Carson lifted his deadly gun, taking aim coolly and ignoring the bullets crackling around him. He felt his hat jerk as a slug plucked at the brim and flattened himself, intent on drawing a bead on the nearest man. He fired and the man fell heavily, blood spurting from a hole blasted in the centre of his chest.

Switching targets, Carson triggered two shots at the second man, sending him diving into cover. He fired a third shot as the man disappeared and the bullet took the rustler in the neck, sending him down in the brush in a splatter of blood.

Carson was ready for the remaining rustler. He heard hoofbeats nearby and raised up to observe. The rustler was riding back out of range, and Carson holstered his sixgun and picked up his rifle. Working the long gun, he fired but missed, and slid the rifle back into its saddle boot. The rustler flattened himself over the horse's neck and spurred the animal mercilessly, riding recklessly in a desperate attempt to get away, and soon disappeared into a dip in the ground and did not reappear.

Carson got to his feet and went forward quickly, sixgun ready once more. He checked the fallen rustlers. One was dead and three others were seriously wounded. He straightened, breathing heavily, disliking the acrid smell of gunsmoke that clung to his nostrils.

Returning to his horse, he swung into the saddle and rode out on the trail of the fleeing rustler, wanting to take the man alive. He followed fresh tracks, and soon spotted the fugitive ahead, spurring his horse mercilessly. Carson let the black run at its own pace and remained on the rustler's tail, far enough back to be out of gunshot range and content to follow.

Reloading his sixgun, Carson kept a close watch on his surroundings. The rustler was easing his horse now, and Carson saw the man glancing back over his shoulder from time to time. Touching spurs to the black, Carson began to close in. The black ran on tirelessly, and, when he was within shooting range, Carson lifted his Colt and fired a shot in the air.

The fleeing rustler glanced over his shoulder then settled lower in his saddle and began to coax his horse into a faster gait. Carson smiled grimly, aware that he had the superior horse, and pushed the black still more to overhaul his quarry. The rustler began following the contours of the undulating range, picking the easier ground for his mount, but the distance between them lessened perceptibly until the rustler suddenly reined in and dived from his saddle, taking his rifle with him.

Carson moved to the left, easing the black into a dip. He kept moving, staying in cover, and then reined in, snatched his Winchester from its boot, and stepped to the ground. Dropping into the lush grass, he bellied up a slope until he could check the ground ahead. His eyes narrowed when he saw the rustler's horse standing with trailing reins, and nearby the rustler's head and shoulders were in plain view amidst a clump of brush.

Carson worked his rifle, levering a shell into the breech. He fired swiftly and his bullet clipped a twig from the brush beside the rustler's head. The man ducked, and Carson took the opportunity to move in several yards. The rustler appeared again, looking for a target, and Carson snapped a shot at him, aiming for a shoulder wound. The man jerked and dropped his rifle. Getting to his feet, Carson went forward, covering the spot where the man had ducked into cover.

'If you got any sense you'll throw out your gun and give up,' Carson yelled.

The man's head appeared some twenty yards away and his sixgun hammered, sending five shots in Carson's direction. Carson went to ground, and when the fusillade was over he got up and closed in, moving at an angle, gun ready. He saw the top of the man's Stetson and covered it, and, when the man arose again and brought his Colt into view, Carson fired swiftly. The bullet hit the man in the centre of the forehead, sending him sprawling backwards with outflung arms.

Gun echoes faded slowly as Carson walked up to the rustler. He gazed unemotionally at the inert body, his eyes narrowed. The man was dead. Carson reloaded his gun and holstered it. Looking around, he was surprised to see a cluster of ranch buildings off to the right and spotted movement in that direction. Two riders were coming fast towards him, and Carson prepared for further trouble. If this was Mabry's ranch then he could expect nothing but hostility from its occupants.

He walked back to where the black was standing and drew his Winchester.

The riders came up fast, guns out, and Carson covered them as they reined in. One was short and middle-aged, the other younger, in his twenties.

'What's going on?' demanded the older man. 'What are you doing on my range?'

'Who are you?' Carson countered.

'Ben Hesp. This is Bar H range.'

Carson lifted the lapel of his leather vest to reveal his law badge. 'I'm Matt Carson. I've just busted a gang of rustlers who were running off your herd.'

Hesp stepped down out of his saddle and trailed his reins, clearly shocked by the news, and Carson gave him the bare details. Hesp turned to his younger companion. 'Dave, go get the crew and bring 'em fast.'

The cowhand nodded and wheeled his mount, raising dust as he departed. Hesp held out his hand to Carson.

'I don't know how to thank you, Marshal,' he said. 'I've been losing considerable stock over the past months. And you've nailed six of the rustlers?'

'There should be one rustler alive and wounded at Mabry's line shack back in that direction.' Carson pointed to the west. 'I tangled with five of them about three miles back and four of them are down in the grass there.' He indicated the dead rustler nearby. 'This one had the chance to quit but wouldn't.'

'How'd you get on to them?' Hesp demanded. 'My crew has been running itself ragged trying to catch them.'

'I ain't got the time to go into that now,' Carson responded. 'I need to get back to that line shack and take the wounded rustler on to Cattle Creek.'

'You're bleeding,' Hesp observed. 'Are you hurt bad?'

'It's OK. I'll make it back to town. Will you collect the bodies of the rustlers and tote them into Cattle Creek?'

'Sure thing! You can rely on it. Do you need someone to ride with you?'

'No thanks. I can handle my end of it.' Carson turned to his horse and swung into the saddle. He paused for a moment, looking around, then lifted a hand to Hesp. 'See you when you make it to town,' he said, and turned back the way he had come.

He rode steadily, and was nearing the line shack from which the rustlers had set out at dawn when he heard the rapid beat of approaching hooves. Riding into cover, he eased his Colt in its holster and prepared for action. The next moment a rider went by at a gallop, and Carson rode out and started in pursuit, for it was Dora Hand.

He glanced back over his shoulder as he rode to catch up with the girl, wondering at her haste. Her back trail appeared to be deserted. He pushed hard. Dora was not looking around, and her haste warned Carson that something was amiss.

He drew his gun and fired a shot skywards. Dora twisted quickly, and it took her some moments to recognise him. Then she pulled her horse to a sli'thering halt and turned to face him.

'I was riding to find you,' she gasped. 'Ham Johnson showed up at the shack before me and Pa could ride out. We wasted time tending that wounded rustler. Johnson shot Pa but I managed to get away, and all I could think of was finding you. I think my pa is dead. Johnson will be on my trail now.'

'Let's turn back,' said Carson. 'I was on my way to the shack. So Johnson's on the loose again, huh? Now how'd he manage to get out of jail?'

'The sheriff turned him loose, of course.' Dora was grimfaced, pale and trembling.

'Rourke is no great shakes as a lawman, but I doubt he would deliberately turn a prisoner loose,' Carson said.

'Don't you believe it! Rourke is in the back pocket of the man running the crooked deals in this county.'

Carson fell silent as they rode, and watched the trail ahead for signs of trouble. When the line shack came into view he reined in and dismounted.

'You better stay here in cover while I go in and take a look around,' he said, trailing his reins.

Dora nodded. Carson dismounted and went through the brush. He saw four horses in the pole corral and figured that Johnson was in the shack. His expression hardened when he saw the figure of Joe Hand sprawled in front of the door of the building.

Moving to the right, he gained the side of the shack and looked for a gap in the boards. He spotted a knot-hole and peered through it into the dim interior of the building. The rustler he had shot was lying on a bunk, and Ham Johnson was sitting at the rough table, eating food.

Carson walked around the back of the shack and along the farther side. He drew his Colt and approached the door, walking in on Johnson, who froze at his appearance.

'I'm getting a mite tired of arresting you and throwing you in jail,' Carson said. 'How'd you get out this time?'

'I told you they can't hold me in town,' Johnson rasped. His face was blotched with bruises and his eyes narrowed as he took in Carson's ominous figure. 'And you should have quit the county while you had the chance. There'll be men out after you now, and they won't stop till you're dead.'

'How'd you get out 've jail?' Carson repeated.

'Why don't you take me back and find out?'

'That's just what I aim to do. On your feet and lift your hands.'

Johnson arose, grinning as he raised his hands. Carson went forward, his gun levelled, and snaked Johnson's gun from its holster.

'Is Joe Hand dead?' Carson demanded.

'He sure is. That's the way we handle his kind.'

'OK, let's go. And don't give me an excuse to blast you, Johnson. You've come to the end of your rope, mister.'

Johnson shrugged and walked to the door. Carson watched him closely, ready for tricks, and stayed back out of arm's length. At that moment the wounded man on the bunk called out, and when Carson glanced at him he saw a sixgun in the man's hand, covering him.

Without hesitation, Carson threw himself sideways to the rough dirt floor. The rustler fired and Carson heard the crackle of the slug as it narrowly passed his head. He landed on his back, gunhand lifting, and snapped two shots at the wounded man. The rustler jerked and dropped his gun, and Carson swung to cover Johnson, temporarily deafened by the hammering shots at close quarters.

Johnson was diving out through the doorway and Carson snapped a shot at the man, hitting him in the back of the thigh. Johnson staggered, fell, and dived to one side, disappearing from Carson's sight. Carson sprang up and followed, and, as he cleared the doorway, Johnson stepped forward and swung his right hand towards Carson.

Sunlight glinted on the blade in Johnson's hand and Carson swung his Colt to connect with the hand. The barrel of the weapon cracked against Johnson's wrist and the knife went flying. Carson swung his left fist and caught Johnson's jaw, staggering the big man. Johnson grabbed at Carson's gunhand, secured a grip on his wrist, and began to wrestle for possession of the gun.

Carson kneed Johnson in the groin and the big man twisted and went over backwards, dragging Carson with him. Carson fell awkwardly and half rolled away. Johnson swarmed towards him, having somehow retrieved the knife he had dropped. He lunged with the long blade and Carson threw himself aside, landing flat on his back. The point of the knife dug into the dirt only an inch or so from his throat, and Carson prepared for a struggle.

Johnson was desperate. He reared up, swinging the knife, and at that moment a gun blasted.

Johnson jerked and cried out, then dropped the knife. He sprawled forward across Carson, who thrust him aside and arose quickly. Looking around, Carson saw Dora only feet away, kneeling beside her dead father, and she was holding a smoking sixgun.

Dora threw down the gun and lifted her hands to her face. Carson, his shoulders heaving, rolled Johnson on to his back. The man was dead, and Carson sighed and went to Dora, grasping her shoulders and lifting her to her feet.

'Thanks, Dora,' he said. 'Johnson had it coming.'

'He shot Pa in cold blood!' she sobbed.

'We'll ride back to town.' Carson spoke quietly. 'I'll saddle the horses in the corral and we'll take the bodies in.'

Dora remained crouched by her father while Carson prepared to return to town. He checked on the wounded rustler in the shack and found him dead. Roping the bodies to their saddles, he pushed Dora into her saddle and they rode out, heading for Cattle Creek.

It was a long, silent ride to town, and, when they finally reached the outskirts, the sun was way past its zenith and the heat of late afternoon was shimmering around them. Carson reined in.

'Dora, I need your evidence to help me clean up around here,' he said, 'but we got to keep you in the background or you could wind up dead like your pa. Is there somewhere you can lay low until I get a few things straight?'

'What's wrong with the jail?' she countered. 'I should be safe in there. Now Pa is dead I want these badmen to pay for what they've done. I'll tell you everything I know, and I'll stand up in court and put the deadwood on Mabry and his gang.'

'OK.' Carson resumed riding, and they entered the main street and rode to the law office.

The town was quiet at this time of the day, but their progress was noted before they reached the jail and several townsmen began to drift along the sidewalks, intent on learning what had happened. Carson dismounted in front of the jail and wrapped his reins around the hitch rail. He grasped Dora's arm when she slid out of her saddle and hurried her across the sidewalk and into the law office.

Shap Newman was lounging at the desk, and looked up when the door opened. Carson palmed his gun and covered him. Newman sprang to his feet, reaching for his holstered gun, then froze under the menace of Carson's weapon

'What's going on?' Newman demanded.

'Mebbe you can tell me,' Carson said. 'Where's Rourke?'

'He rode out for Prescott last night.'

'I got Johnson face down on a horse outside. How'd he get out of jail again?'

'Someone tied a rope to the back window in the cells and yanked the bars out. There was a horse waiting for Johnson.'

'Who just happened to be in the cell with the window, huh?' Carson rapped.

Newman was gazing at the ashen-faced Dora. 'What's she doing here?' he demanded. 'I had a report last night that she'd gone missing.'

'He's one of them,' Dora said. 'He was in Mabry's gang down in Texas.'

'That's what I figured.' Carson motioned with his gun. 'Get your hands up, Newman, and turn around.'

Newman looked as if he wanted to argue, but shrugged and turned away. Carson snaked the man's gun from its holster and then picked up the cell keys.

'Take off the law badge, put it on the desk, then get moving,' he rapped. 'You know where the cells are.'

Newman removed the badge and tossed it on the desk. Carson locked him in a cell and returned to the office to find Ash Norton and three townsmen standing on the threshold. Dora was sitting at the desk, her face in her hands.

'What's going on, Marshal?' asked the saloon-man. 'I saw you coming along the street with dead men across their saddles. Is there anything I can do to help?' He paused, then added, 'Say, you've got blood on your shirt! Have you been hurt?'

'It's nothing.' Carson explained what had occurred.

Norton shook his head. 'Trust Rourke to leave when he did,' he growled. 'He must have known there was action coming up.'

'I'll get round to the sheriff later,' Carson promised. 'Is there anyone around here I can trust to keep the peace in town while I'm bringing in the badmen?'

'I'll use a couple of my own men,' Norton said.

Carson smiled. 'How do I know I can trust you?' he countered. 'I'm a stranger here, and I've killed a deputy sheriff because he was crooked and thrown your town marshal in jail because he's an outlaw from Texas. So who can I trust?'

'You've jailed Newman!' Norton shook his head in disbelief. 'So you've got to take a chance on someone,' he said. 'You've got no choice but to try me. I'll stand by here with a couple of my men while you do what you figure is necessary around town. Is there anyone else you're planning to arrest?' He crossed to the desk, picked up the law badge that Newman had discarded, and pinned it to his vest. 'We can dispense with the formalities for now.'

Carson nodded. 'OK. I got to trust someone. Dora is gonna be an important witness when I bring the badmen to trial and I figure her life could be in danger. I want her kept in protective custody until the situation around here clears. She's done nothing wrong so she's not under arrest. But guard her.'

'She'll be here in one piece whenever you want her,' said Norton. 'There's a room back there she can use.'

'Is Mabry or any of his men still around town?'

'Mabry rode back to his ranch last night but he left Wiley and Raynor in town. Raynor ain't been around today, but Wiley is in my saloon now.'

'I'll pick up Wiley,' Carson mused, 'then I'll get something to eat. I wanta ride out to Mabry's place soon as I can. I've made a breakthrough around here. Are there some local men who can be trusted to ride out as a posse? I'll need gun help to bring matters to a head.'

'Leave it to me,' Norton nodded. 'I'll have a dozen men standing by to ride out when you're ready.'

'Thanks. Perhaps you'll take care of the dead men out there, and stable my black for me.'

'Don't worry about a thing,' Norton assured him. 'I'll handle the details.'

Carson nodded. He had taken all the precautions possible, and wanted to waste no time taking advantage of the situation. He needed to strike before the badmen realized what was going on, and with a little luck he could have the whole business settled without further bloodshed.

NINE

Carson stifled a yawn as he went along the sidewalk to locate Wiley. He checked Norton's saloon but there was no sign of Mabry's gunman, and, noting that the bartender seemed nervous, he remained alert as he paused just inside the batwings and looked around.

'Where's Wiley?' he demanded.

'He left in a hurry when he saw you riding along the street with dead men across their saddles,' replied the bartender.

Carson left hurriedly, and watched his surroundings closely as he made for the stable. Frank Larter was in his office, and Carson checked the barn for Wiley. Failing to see the gunman, he returned to the office.

'Have you seen Wiley?' he demanded.

'He got his horse a few minutes ago and went out of here like a bat outa hell!' replied Larter.

Carson grimaced. He had hoped to ride into Mabry's ranch unexpectedly, but that seemed out of the question now. 'I'll need a fresh horse shortly,' he said. 'My black will be brought in. Take care of it, huh?'

'Sure thing, and you can use the chestnut down

at the far end on the right. It's the kind of horse you need for chasing badmen. It'll run anything around here into the ground.'

'Thanks.' Carson could feel tiredness creeping into his mind. He stifled a yawn. 'I'll be back for the chestnut in about thirty minutes.'

He turned away and went back along the street to the eating house. Food was essential right now, and there was no point in hurrying if Wiley was riding hell for leather with a warning for Mabry.

'Matt!' Joel Carson appeared on the sidewalk. 'Hi! I'm just out of school and I heard all the talk outside the jail. You killed Ham Johnson and got some rustlers. Have you found out who killed my pa?'

'Not yet, but we'll get there. I'm on my way to eat. I'll be riding out later.'

'They're saying at the jail that Cal Mabry is a rustler,' Joel added. 'When I came out've school I saw Wiley riding out of town, headed for Mabry's place.'

'Yeah, I heard. I'll be seeing Wiley later, I guess.' Carson looked around quickly when he heard the sound of hooves on the street, and saw a man leading his black and the horses loaded with the bodies of Joe Hand, Johnson and the rustler.

'I'm taking these to the undertaker,' the man reported, 'and I'll put your hoss in the stable. Is there anything else I can do for you, Marshal?'

'Tell Larter to put my gear on that chestnut he said I could borrow,' Carson said, and the man went on his way.

Carson went on to Brice's restaurant, accompanied by Joel, but the boy halted outside.

'I've got things to do, Matt,' he said. 'See you later.'

'Don't get into trouble,' Carson said as the boy darted away. He entered the restaurant to find Annie seated at a table with Frank Brice. They were drinking coffee, having cleaned up after the noon rush. Annie sprang to her feet, almost upsetting a coffee cup in her haste.

'Matt!' she gasped, her expression showing worry. 'I was beginning to think something bad had happened to you. I went to the hotel early this morning and the clerk said you were asleep and not to be disturbed for anything. Then Frank Larter came in here at noon and whispered to me that you rode out of town last night but no one should know.'

Carson nodded and sat down. 'Everything is fine,' he said. 'I need food, and I don't have much time. I'm riding out with a posse shortly. By the way, Ham Johnson is dead! He won't bother you any more.'

Annie's face paled, and Carson smiled reassuringly.

'He had it coming,' he said, 'and he sure asked for it. He was busted out of jail again last night, so I heard.'

'I'll get you something to eat.' Annie hurried into the kitchen, and Carson sat down opposite Frank Brice with a sigh of relief.

'You feel like talking now?' he demanded. 'I've made a breakthrough in this crooked business, and it'll soon be finished.'

'I've got nothing to say until you've slammed the jail door on all those responsible,' Brice replied harshly.

'Which means there are some badmen to be uncovered here in town, huh?' Carson nodded. 'I don't figure the rustlers killed Lon because he had nothing to do with law dealing outside of town limits, but that can wait. There's some tidying up to be done out on the range. When that's finished I'll turn my attention to Cattle Creek.'

Annie returned with a filled plate of food and Carson ate hungrily, his mind on what had to be done. Annie brought him coffee and a large slice of apple pie. When he had finished, Annie bathed and bandaged his shoulder.

'Thanks,' he said. 'I've got to be riding now. See you later.' He went out to the sidewalk, and Joel stepped forward.

'I been waiting for you to finish, Matt,' he said softly. 'I've been looking round the town, and Wiley ain't left. Leastways, he did, but he must have doubled back. His horse is in some bushes back of the church, and Wiley is waiting in a disused barn back there. It looks like he's waiting to get at you, Matt.'

'Thanks, Joel. You better go to your mother now and stay with her, huh? I'll check up on Wiley.'

'Don't take any chances with him,' the boy warned. 'He's a hardcase, Matt.'

Carson patted the boy's shoulder. 'It's OK,' he said. 'I got a job to do and I better get to it.'

He went along the sidewalk towards the church. There was a crowd of townsmen standing outside the law office and he planned to cut down the next alley to avoid them, wanting to approach Wiley's position from the rear. He watched his surroundings as he walked, and almost immediately spotted a furtive movement in an alley mouth opposite.

A gun flamed and Carson threw himself flat on the sidewalk with a bullet crackling in his ear. He rolled off the sidewalk into the dust of the street, palming his Colt. Lifting his gun, he returned fire instantly, and a second gun blasted at him from another point across the street.

Realizing that he had walked into a gun trap, Carson slithered under the edge of the sidewalk, and bullets splintered through the woodwork above his head as the ambushers bracketed the area. He held his fire, intent on extricating himself from the trap. The shooting suddenly stopped. It was a hit or miss affair for the ambushers. They could not loiter around the scene of the shooting. Carson's mind worked swiftly. He guessed Wiley was one of the men involved, and needed to catch him. Crawling sideways, he reached the alley and headed along it to the back lots, mindful of Joel's information about Wiley's horse being in bushes at the back of the church. Silence had returned, although the sounds of the shooting remained inside his head. His gun was clutched in his right hand. He reached the back lots and kept to the rear of the buildings fronting the street as he ran swiftly towards the back of the church. He was tensed for more action, and, nearing the church, stepped into cover and checked out his surroundings. He saw the bushes Joel mentioned and made for them, gun ready, and a sigh of disappointment escaped him when he found no sign of a tethered horse. Wiley had shot at him from the far side of the street, and the gunman would not want to be too far away from his only means of escape.

Carson went back to the stable to find that Larter had readied the chestnut for him. He led the animal outside and swung into the saddle, riding along the street until he reached Ash Norton and a dozen townsmen, who were looking around.

'What was all the shooting about?' demanded Norton.

'I figure it was Wiley, and someone was helping him.' Carson's tone was steady. 'I reckon he's lit out for Maybry's ranch now, and I wanta be on his heels when he gets there. Send some men after me soon as they can get mounted. Just point me in the general direction of Mabry's place.'

'Ride out of town to the north and take the first fork west,' Norton said. 'There'll be a dozen men riding behind you within minutes.'

Carson nodded and touched spurs to the chestnut, scattering the townsmen as he set off along the street. He left town at a fast clip, and began to breathe easier as he moved along the open trail. A mile out of town he took a turnoff that led to the west. He saw two sets of fresh tracks on the trail and peered ahead, nodding to himself when he spotted a pair of riders far ahead, galloping across the undulating range. He settled down to ride hard and fast, and grinned when he found that Larter had not been exaggerating when he bragged about the chestnut's speed and endurance. He began slowly and surely to close up on his quarry.

An hour later he was close enough to the two riders to be able to recognise one of them as Wiley. He loosened his Colt in its holster, mindful of the fact that he could easily ride into an ambush. The thought had hardly entered his mind when a gun crashed from ahead and a bullet whined over his head. He flattened himself in his saddle almost before the echoes began to roll and touched spurs to the chestnut. The horse surged into a gallop and Carson headed straight towards the two men, who had reined in. He saw Wiley turn and ride off fast, but the second man dismounted, rifle in hand, and dropped into cover. The next instant he was firing at Carson, who hunkered a little lower in his saddle and pushed the chestnut harder, cocking his gun and holding it ready for action. The gunman was shooting frantically but poorly, and Carson closed in swiftly, taking advantage of the ground to throw the man off aim.

His precipitate action affected the gunman, whose shooting became ragged. and Carson quickly drew within sixgun range and began to reply, his accurate fire causing the man to duck and stay down. He was only yards from the spot where the man was crouching when the man sprang up and ran towards his waiting horse. Raising his gun, Carson fired instantly, blinking against the flaring smoke as the weapon crashed. The rider fell, and Carson hoped he had not killed him.

He went forward, gun cocked, covering the figure lying on the ground. Stepping down from his saddle, Carson approached the fallen man, ready for tricks. But there was no movement, and when he was close enough to check he found the man was dead, hit between the shoulder blades.

Sitting back on his heels, Carson breathed

deeply of the keen breeze blowing into his face, making his eyes water. He looked at the dead man's face and narrowed his eyes, for he was looking at a total stranger.

Hooves sounded off to Carson's right and he stood up and looked around, spotting a rider coming quickly towards him. It was not Wiley, but he did not relax, and, when the newcomer approached, Carson was surprised when he recognised Sheriff Rourke.

The sheriff arrived, breathless and cursing fitfully.

'I heard you'd ridden back to Prescott,' Carson observed.

'That's what I said back in town, but I needed to take a look around the range and try to find out what's happening,' Rourke said. He looked as if he hadn't slept in a week, and his unshaven face seemed grey under its coating of dust.

'And what have you discovered?' Carson demanded.

The sheriff shrugged, shaking his head. 'Nary a thing.'

'Then you've been looking in all the wrong places.' Carson explained what he had done in the past twenty-four hours. 'Now I'm riding to Mabry's place. Wiley is heading there.'

'I'll ride with you,' Rourke said. 'But I can't believe that Mabry is a Texas outlaw.'

'Take a look at this man and tell me who he is,' said Carson.

'Is he dead?' demanded Rourke.

'They usually die when I shoot them.' Carson's voice was harsh. 'Take a look at him.'

Rourke bent over the lifeless figure, stared at the dead man's features, then cursed fitfully.

'Well?' rapped Carson.

'It's Bat Morgan.'

'And who in hell is Bat Morgan?'

'He works for Cal Mabry.'

Carson shook his head. 'I guess there's only one way to find out what's going on,' he mused, 'and that's at Mabry's place.'

'Hell, if Mabry is what you say he is then we can't just ride in there. That would be asking for trouble. We'd need a posse to back us.'

'There should be one on its way from town,' Carson said.

'You're really getting at this business,' Rourke nodded. 'OK, you handle it. I'll come along for the ride.'

They mounted and continued. Carson gazed around the silent range, watching their surroundings, and, when they eventually topped a rise, he was relieved to see a sprawl of ranch buildings lying in a narrow valley. Night was almost upon them and shadows were creeping in, cutting down their vision.

'Mabry's place,' said Rourke.

Carson saw an oblong of light shining from the dark pile of the ranch house. 'I'll sneak in to see what's going on,' he said. 'I figure Wiley has warned Mabry what's happened in town, and if Mabry has found out that his rustlers have been eliminated then he'll either pull out or make plans to stop me.'

'He won't pull out,' Rourke asserted. 'He's got too much going for him. We better wait for the posse to show.'

Carson shook his head and went forward slowly, anxious not to warn the occupants of the ranch of his presence. A faint trail led down to the ranch buildings and he followed it at little more than a walk. Reaching a small stand of trees about fifty yards out from the ranch house, he swung out of the saddle and tethered his mount in cover. Rourke did the same, and followed Carson as he moved in on foot.

Carson spotted a horse standing at a rail in front of the house and figured it belonged to Wiley. Moving to the porch, he was intent on getting to the lighted window to see what was going on in the house. When a sun-warped board creaked loudly under his foot he froze in his tracks and motioned for Rourke to remain in the background. The sheriff faded into the shadows.

Moving forward again, Carson gained the front wall of the house and eased against it, then edged sideways until he could take a look through the uncurtained window. He saw Wiley inside, sitting in a big easy chair and swigging from a bottle. There was no sign of Mabry.

Before he could consider his next action, Carson sensed a faint movement at his side and then the muzzle of a gun dug against his side.

'Don't move,' a harsh voice warned. 'You so much as take a deep breath and I'll gutshoot you.'

Carson stood still, his breath catching in his throat. He felt a hand jerk his sixgun out of his holster.

'That's better,' the guard continued. 'And seeing you're so interested in what's going inside the house you can go in and find out.' He rapped on the window with the muzzle of his gun and shouted: 'Hey, Wiley, you got company. Come on out and take a look.'

Carson moved swiftly, aware that for a brief moment the guard's gun was not covering him. He half turned towards the man and struck shrewdly, his fist crashing against an unprotected jaw. The man sprawled instantly, and Carson snatched back his Colt and straightened. Glancing through the window, he saw Wiley on his feet already running to the door of the room.

Carson did not hesitate. He had to gamble on doing the right thing. Lunging for the front door, he shouldered it open and plunged across the threshold, gun lifted and ready for action.

TEN

Wiley appeared from the room on the right when Carson was still two strides from its door, and the man pulled up short at the sight of Carson's ominous figure. He reached for his gun, but was not quick enough for Carson kept moving, swinging his sixgun. He slammed the barrel against Wiley's skull and the man crumpled instantly. Carson jerked the man's sixgun from its holster and hurled it out of reach.

He looked towards the doorway as a movement caught his eye and Rourke appeared. Wiley groaned, and Carson saw the man was only semi-conscious.

'Get him up, Sheriff,' Carson ordered, 'and let's hear what he's got to say.'

Rourke slapped Wiley's face and the man opened his eyes. 'On your feet,' the sheriff rasped. He helped Wiley up and thrust him into a chair.

Carson moved in and confronted Wiley. 'You ambushed me in town,' he rapped.

'It wasn't serious,' Wiley shook his head, dazed by the blow he had received. 'I did it to liven up your nosin' around. Nothing was happening in town, and I figgered a few shots would help move things along.'

'And you left Morgan on the trail to finish me off.'

'I figured you might get rough if you caught up with me.' Wiley fingered the bruise forming above his left ear. 'I told Morgan to delay you till dark, then fade into the night.'

'You're lying.' Carson spoke harshly. 'That shooting was for real.'

'There ain't no harm done,' Wiley protested.

'Is that what you'll tell the coroner at Morgan's inquest?' Carson demanded.

'His inquest?' Riley stiffened. 'You killed him?'

'He's dead. Sheriff, Wiley is going to jail. Put your cuffs on him and start back to town. Wiley, where's Mabry?'

Wiley shrugged. 'I got no idea. I expected him to be here.'

'Fetch in that guard, Sheriff. He should be awake now.'

Rourke went out and returned a moment later with the guard Carson had slugged. The man was unsteady, his eyes showing that he was feeling the effects of the blow he had been dealt.

'What's your name and where's Mabry?' Carson asked.

'I'm Talman. Mabry rode out a couple of hours ago. One of the crew came in and they left together. Mabry didn't say where he was going. He told me to look after the place. There's no one else around.'

Rourke handcuffed the prisoners and ushered them out. Carson followed. A horse was saddled for the guard and both prisoners were made to mount up. The sheriff led them to the stand of trees where his and Carson's horses were tethered.

'I'm not going back to town with you,' Carson said softly. 'I need to do some more checking out here. Can you get these two to jail without trouble?'

'Sure,' Rourke nodded. 'But you better watch your step. Something bad is going on, and now you've horned in you could get more than you bargain for.'

'Just get these two back to jail,' Carson said. 'I'll handle this end of it.'

Rourke tied a short length of rope to the bridles of his two prisoners and wrapped the loose end around his saddlehorn. He swung into his saddle and moved out, leading the prisoners. Carson watched the trio until they faded into the night, and a sense of loneliness assailed him when their hoofbeats faded and full silence ensued. He readied his horse for travel and swung into the saddle, then sat and looked around the deserted ranch, peering into the dense shadows. He drew a deep breath, his thoughts profound. Had Mabry pulled out for good? Would he cut his losses and run, as he did from Texas, or would he hunt down those who knew his secret to silence them?

The breeze tugged at him and the chestnut moved impatiently. Carson glanced around again. He did not think Mabry was the kind to run at the first signs of danger. He dismounted and led the horse back into the stand of trees, tethering it in cover. It looked like being a long night, and despite the fact that he was tired, he could not afford to sleep.

He stood in the shadows, looking around and

waiting, his mind upon his problems. He still had to discover who killed Lon, and there was no indication yet of the guilty man.

Somewhere out there in the darkness a steel shod hoof struck a stone and Carson came to full alertness. He moved to the chestnut and pressed a hand to the animal's nostrils to prevent it making a noise, and a moment later he heard a horse whinny in the shadows across the yard. Moments later two riders materialized, and Carson watched them cross to the house and dismount.

'Talman, where the hell are you?' one of the men called, and Carson smiled grimly when he recognised Mabry's voice.

'What in hell is going on around here, Mabry?' another voice demanded. 'Where is everyone? Where's the bunch you keep out at that line shack?'

'I told you they're out on a job,' Mabry replied. 'And obviously it's taking them longer than I figured. They'll be back on home range some time tomorrow, I guess. Quit worrying. What can go wrong with this business?'

'That's a federal lawman in town,' the other protested. 'I said you should have left his brother alone. Killing the town marshal wasn't a good idea.'

'I didn't kill him! I was against it myself, come to that. But we can smooth things over. When the gang gets back with that herd we'll ride into town and bury any witness who can give us trouble.'

'You better count Ham Johnson in with them. He's nothing but trouble these days.'

Carson was straining his ears in an attempt to

recognise the voice of the second man. He could identify Mabry's thick tone but the other's quiet voice eluded him.

'I'd better be getting back to town,' the man said. 'The boss is worried, and he wants a full report. That new marshal is giving him the creeps.'

'Tell him to forget about it.' Mabry laughed harshly. 'It's all right for him, living the soft life in town. We're the ones taking all the risks. Tell him I'll be in some time tomorrow to talk to him. I can't do a thing until the gang gets back.'

Carson heard the sound of hooves crossing the yard, and caught an indistinct glimpse of a rider moving out. The man was almost immediately swallowed up in the night, and a few moments later the sounds of his progress faded and silence returned.

Carson found himself in a quandary. He wanted to take Mabry, and he also wanted to follow the unknown man to see who he reported to in town. Mabry had been against the killing of Lon but evidently the man they called the boss had insisted on it. His thoughts ranged far and wide as he watched Mabry dismount at the porch of the house and then enter the building.

Ten minutes later, as Carson was preparing to sneak into the house, Mabry emerged, mounted his horse and rode out, moving at a canter away across the darkened range. Carson quickly fetched the chestnut and followed as closely as he dared, staying back out of earshot but close enough to keep his quarry in sight. Mabry rode steadily, and progressed across the range until, after some three miles, he reached a cabin standing on the bank of a dry creek.

The place, another line shack, was in darkness, but Mabry rode in boldly and shouted to announce his presence, his harsh voice breaking the peacefulness of the night. A light sprang into being inside the cabin, and a moment later three men emerged from the squat building, illuminated by lamplight issuing from the open door at their backs.

Carson had dismounted when the cabin came into view, and stood in cover with his horse. Mabry talked at some length to the men, and Carson was unable to hear what passed between them. Then the trio hurried to a nearby pole corral and saddled their mounts while Mabry swung his horse and started back in the direction of his ranch house.

Carson gripped the flaring nostrils of his horse as Mabry passed by, and the rancher was so close it seemed impossible that he would not detect Carson's presence. But Mabry vanished into the night and Carson began to breathe easier. He watched the three men, and when they moved off from the corral he followed them at a safe distance.

The trio pushed their horses at a fast clip, the sounds of their combined hooves being sufficient to cover the noise made by Carson's mount, and he followed them closely, impatient to discover the nature of their business. They angled to the east of Mabry's ranch. and Carson's sense of direction indicated that they were making for Cattle Creek.

When he thought of Rourke heading for town with two prisoners, Carson began to wonder about

Mabry's intentions. The men he was following were obviously a part of Mabry's crew, and if they were now intent on committing a crime then this could be the break he was hoping for. He stiffened himself against tiredness and forced himself to remain alert.

It was close to dawn when the trio reached Cattle Creek, and they circled the town and approached the jail from the back lots. The greying light bothered Carson, for in a few minutes his cover would evaporate completely and he needed to stay in close contact with these men. He dismounted behind a derelict barn when the three reined up behind the jail, and stood at a corner, watching them intently.

The men dismounted and entered the alley beside the jail.

Carson eased forward on foot, and followed into the alley when he saw the trio leaving their horses in cover at the street end. He hurried along the alley and peered into the street. The men were standing at the door of the jail. One of them was hammering on it and calling for the sheriff.

Carson loosened his Colt in its holster. Tense moments passed, and then the door of the jail was opened and the three men trooped into the office. Carson eased forward to the window and risked a look inside. The three men had drawn their weapons and Rourke was unlocking the door leading into the cells.

Palming his gun, Carson waited until Rourke had entered the cell block followed by two of the men. The third man turned to the street door, and Carson moved in. The door opened and the man emerged. Carson hit him across the forehead with the barrel of his gun and caught the body as it slumped to the sidewalk. He grabbed the man's Colt from its holster and went into the jail.

Crossing to the connecting door, Carson peered into the cell block, his gun levelled. Rourke was unlocking the cell in which Wiley and Talman were locked, and the two men behind the sheriff were holding their guns.

'That will do,' Carson said, earing back the hammer of his gun. 'Relock that door, Sheriff.'

Rourke froze at the sound of Carson's voice. The two men jerked their heads around to look at Carson, and the nearer one instinctively swung his gun in Carson's direction. Carson fired instantly, the shot filling the jail with noise and smoke. His bullet took the man in the chest, the impact throwing him against his companion. Carson stepped forward, gun steady, covering the second man, who was baulked by the wounded man. Both men fell to the floor, and Carson stepped in and grabbed two guns, wrenching one from the grasp of the unwounded man.

'Am I glad to see you!' Rourke gasped, stepping away from the cell. 'These men knocked me up and pulled guns on me. They were figuring to take prisoners out've here.'

'I know what's going on.' Carson handed a gun to the sheriff. 'Cover these while I fetch the third man.'

He went out to the sidewalk. The third man was stirring. Carson dragged him to his feet and led him into the jail. Rourke had opened a cell and the two hardcases were inside, one lying inertly on the floor. Carson thrust the third man into the cell and Rourke slammed the door and locked it. Sweat was beading the sheriff's weatherbeaten face.

'How about the one I shot?' demanded Carson.

'He's dead.' Rourke's tone was callous. 'I'll get the undertaker over shortly. How come you managed to show up right when you was needed?'

Carson explained, eyeing the men in the cell. He brought Rourke up to date on his activities.

'Who are these men?' he asked. 'Are they Mabry's crew?'

'I've never seen 'em before,' replied the sheriff. 'They're strangers to me. Looks like Mabry's got some big explaining to do, huh?'

'What did these men say to you when you opened the door?'

'They told me to turn Johnson loose.'

'So Mabry hadn't got word that Johnson is dead,' Carson mused. 'Did Ben Hesp turn up with the dead rustlers?'

'Yeah. Ash Norton was running things around here when I got back and he said he'd managed to keep that business quiet so as not to alarm the badmen dug in here in town.'

'You got any idea who the badmen might be?' Carson asked. 'I overheard Mabry telling Wiley the night before last that he had to talk to the boss.'

The sheriff shook his head. 'I got no idea who that could be, but I figger you'll flush him out before too long.'

Carson nodded and confronted the two men standing in the cell, their dead pard lying on the ground between them.

'I guess I don't have to tell you that you're in bad trouble, huh?' he demanded. 'Who are you? Do you ride for Mabry?'

Neither man replied, and Carson turned away.

'Let them sweat for awhile,' he told Rourke, and went into the office.

Rourke followed, and locked the door to the cells before dumping the keys on the desk. 'What happens now?' he asked.

'I wish I knew.' Carson stifled a yawn. 'I'm plumb tuckered out, but I don't figure this business can wait even a few hours while I get some sleep. I'd better bring Mabry in. He's got a lot of explaining to do, and he'll know the answers to many of the questions I want answered.'

'I could fetch him,' Rourke said. 'You can't do it all on your own.'

Carson shook his head. 'I'll handle Mabry myself. In the meantime, keep quiet about these developments. I'll have a bite to eat then head back to Mabry's place. You handle this end of the deal, Sheriff. There are three horses in the alley. Have someone take care of them.'

Rourke nodded, and Carson went out to the sidewalk, pausing to breathe deeply of the keen morning air. Full daylight had come, and the sun was beginning to show above the eastern horizon. He took the chestnut to the livery barn and Frank Larter appeared from his office.

'I'll be riding out again in about an hour,' Carson said. 'Have my gear transferred to my black.'

He went on along the street, fighting tiredness, and saw Annie just ahead, making her way to the restaurant. He called and she turned and came hurrying to his side, her face expressing concern.

'I hardly slept last night, thinking that at any moment someone would come and tell me you had been killed,' she said.

'You don't have to worry about me,' he said tiredly. 'Can I get some breakfast? I've got a long day ahead.'

'Sure. What have you been doing? By the look of you I'd say you didn't get any sleep last night.'

'You're right, and I have to move fast now.' Carson glanced around as the sound of hooves reached his ears. He saw a rider approaching, and moved fast when he caught the glint of sunlight on a drawn weapon in the man's hand. The rider spurred forward when he realized he had been spotted, and Carson flowed into action. He thrust Annie aside and dropped to one knee on the boardwalk, his sixgun in his hand.

The rider bent low in his saddle, shouting to spur on his horse, his voice echoing in the early morning. He levelled his pistol and began shooting, and Carson gritted his teeth as slugs hammered around him. Ignoring the flying lead, he drew a bead on the speeding rider and thumbed off a shot that crashed raucously, filled with relief despite his tension because the outlaws he was fighting had obviously decided to come out into the open against him, and that meant they were worried.

ELEVEN

Carson's single shot took the rider in the chest and the man reared back in his saddle before pitching sideways to fall heavily into the dust. He bounced and rolled as the horse galloped on, then lay inertly on his back, arms outflung, blood spreading over the front of his shirt.

Carson got to his feet, alert for further trouble, his gun cocked and ready for action. He saw Otto Kunkel standing in the doorway of the store, already dressed in a white apron. There were other signs of early morning activity along the street, but nothing to arouse suspicion in Carson's mind. He uncocked his gun and exhaled deeply as he holstered the weapon.

Annie was lying on the sidewalk where he had thrust her, and for a moment Carson thought she had been hit by one of the flying slugs. But she was merely dazed, and her face was pale with shock as she began to stir. Carson helped her to her feet.

'Are you OK, Annie?' he demanded.

She nodded, leaning against him for support while struggling to overcome her shock.

'Matt!' she gasped. 'Is it always like this for you?'

'Don't worry about it.' He smiled grimly. 'Will you look at this galoot? I need to know who he is and who his friends are.'

She nodded, her lips compressed, and moved towards the inert figure sprawled in the dust. Carson supported her with a powerful hand under her right elbow. He had seen at a glance that the man was dead. Annie looked at the immobile face then turned away, her features ashen.

'I've never seen him before,' she said as they regained the sidewalk. 'He's a stranger, Matt.'

'Why would a stranger take a shot at me?' mused Carson. He patted her arm. 'Go on to the restaurant. I'll need breakfast shortly so have it ready for me.'

She nodded and hurried away. Carson looked around and saw Rourke coming along the sidewalk. He shook his head slowly, considering the situation. If someone was bringing in strangers to do their dirty work it meant that they needed to keep their actions secret.

Rourke arrived at a run. Sweat was streaking his face. He could not speak for some moments, and stood over the dead man, studying the immobile features.

'Well?' Carson demanded at length. 'Any idea who he is?'

Rourke shook his head. 'He's a stranger,' he wheezed.

Hooves thudding along the street caught Carson's attention and he turned to see a rider cantering towards them. The man drew abreast and slid out of the saddle.

'I heard the shooting, and came out of my cabin in time to stop this runaway,' he explained, his eyes on the dead man.

Carson walked around the horse, examining it, and saw the CM brand on its rump.

'That's one of Cal Mabry's nags,' Rourke said.

Carson nodded. 'So what's a stranger doing with it?'

'I'd sure like to know.' Rourke scratched his head.

Carson shrugged. 'I'm calling on Mabry this morning. I've got enough evidence to jail him. I'll take this horse along.'

'Sure.' Rourke took the reins of the horse. 'He'll be waiting for you at the livery barn. I'll warn the undertaker he's got some business out here, huh?'

Carson nodded and turned away, heading for the restaurant. He saw Joel Carson standing on the sidewalk near the eating house, and the boy came running forward.

'I heard the shooting, Matt. Ma said someone tried to get you. I wish you'd been around before pa was killed. He'd have had more chance with you siding him.'

'You can help me, Joel,' Carson said. 'Cut along to the stable and watch for anyone riding out of town between now and the time I come for my horse. Will you do that?'

'Sure thing. Can I ride with you today?'

'Nope. It's likely to be dangerous. Don't let anyone know you're watching the stable. OK?'

'I'm always hanging around there. Folks are used to seeing me,' Joel grinned and hurried away.

Carson was thoughtful as he ate the breakfast

Annie prepared for him. He hurried it, for he needed to be on the trail, and afterwards, with Annie's good wishes ringing in his ears, he went back to the stable to find his black ready for travel.

'There ain't been anyone down here for a horse,' reported Joel.

'Good. That's what I hoped to hear.' Carson collected the Mabry horse, mounted his own and rode out. He lifted a hand to the excited Joel and cantered out of town, his thoughts ranging far ahead as he hit the trail to Mabry's spread. He had more than enough to work on although he was as yet no nearer to his brother's killer. But someone would start talking now the chips were down, and he was content with the way the situation was progressing.

He remained alert, and reached Mabry's ranch without incident. Reining up in the grove of trees which had sheltered his horse during the previous night, he studied the ranch buildings. The place looked deserted, and he compressed his lips. It didn't look good. Someone should be around handling the chores.

He eased out of the trees and, keeping out of sight of the ranch, made a detour to approach the house from the rear. He figured Mabry should be here at least until he knew whether the attack in town had been successful or not. He left the horses tethered some distance out and moved in on foot, getting down on his belly to cover the last yards to the rear of the house. Silence pressed in around him and he moved slowly, intent on maintaining surprise.

The sound of a horse entering the yard out front alerted him and he passed the rear of the house, moving along the side to the front corner to ease forward into a position that gave him a view of the yard. He saw a rider coming in openly, and narrowed his eyes in an attempt to identify the newcomer. The man was dressed in a store suit and was not openly wearing a gun. Carson frowned as he awaited developments. The rider came straight to the house and reined up at the porch.

'Hello!' he called, his voice echoing in the silence. He did not dismount, and sat waiting impatiently for a reply. When none came he dismounted, walked on to the porch and hammered on the door with his fist. 'Anyone to home?' He turned and looked around the yard, hands on his hips, shaking his head when it became apparent that there would be no answer to his summons.

Carson looked around the yard, and tensed when he suddenly spotted the muzzle of a rifle poking through a hole in the hayloft of the barn. His breath caught in his throat and he froze, wondering if he had been spotted. Easing backwards, he drew his Colt, thankful now that he had not ridden in boldly.

The newcomer returned to his horse, mounted and began to ride away, and at that moment a tall, unkempt figure emerged from the barn, rifle in hand. Carson noted that the rifle in the hayloft was still showing and awaited developments.

'Hey, Pendle!' called the man in the barn doorway. 'What you doin' out here?'

'Spanton!' The rider dismounted as the man approached. 'Why are you skulking in the barn? You expecting trouble?'

'I got orders to be careful. What's your problem?' Spanton lowered the muzzle of his rifle as he approached. 'You want Mabry, huh? Well he ain't here. He rode out before dawn.'

'When he gets back tell him the man he sent to town got hisself killed this morning and the marshal is still alive.'

'I told Mabry that Traske was useless with a gun. But Cal half expected it, I figure. He said if word came through while he was gone that Traske didn't manage to kill Carson then Fargo will have to go in and make his play.' Spanton turned to the barn and yelled: 'Hey, Fargo, come on out. You got a job to do.'

Carson saw the muzzle of the rifle in the hayloft disappear, and a moment later a short, fleshy man emerged from the barn and came sauntering across the yard, rifle in hand.

'Traske is dead,' Spanton told him. 'You got to ride into town and make your play, Fargo.'

'Heck, I told Cal to let me go in the first place.' The short man was cold-eyed, and he turned instantly to go to the corral. 'I'll saddle up and ride back to town with you, Pendle,' he flung back over his shoulder.

Carson remained motionless, hoping to learn more, but Pendle rode out slowly, leaving Spanton standing on the porch, rifle in the crook of his left arm. Fargo saddled up and came back across the yard at a canter. He lifted a hand to Spanton and kept going, moving fast to catch up with the now distant Pendle.

Spanton stood on the porch until the riders disappeared, then turned to enter the house. Carson stepped into view at that moment, sixgun in hand, and Spanton, catching his movement, froze in mid-step, curbing an instinct to level his rifle.

'Try it if you want,' advised Carson. 'But I need to talk to you. Make your move or drop it.'

Spanton dropped the rifle and raised his hands.

'Anyone else on the place?' asked Carson.

'Not now.' Spanton stood motionless.

Carson moved in and dug his muzzle against Spanton's belly while he removed a holstered sixgun from the man. Then he stepped away and motioned for Spanton to sit on the porch steps while he stood with his back to the wall of the house, watching his surroundings.

'Do you know who I am?' Carson demanded.

'I ain't never set eyes on you before.'

'You just sent Fargo into town to kill me.' Carson smiled at the man's shock. 'Looks like you're in bad trouble, mister, seeing that I'm a deputy U.S. marshal.'

'I ain't done nothing against the law,' growled Spanton.

'OK. So you're an honest man. Then you'll be pleased to answer my questions, huh?'

Spanton did not reply, and Carson cocked his gun, the clicks sounding ominous in the silence. Spanton became apprehensive, his face showing signs of fear.

'You should be feeling scared,' Carson rasped. 'I'm looking for the man who killed my brother and I ain't concerned about the law in that business. It's personal, and I'm gonna handle it aside from my law work.'

'I don't know who killed your brother.'

'But you know about Mabry stealing cattle, huh? So give me details.'

'All I know is Mabry rode out at dawn.'

Carson's patience was exhausted. He waggled his gun. 'OK. On your feet. We're riding into town. I can get Mabry later. There's a horse waiting for you back of the house. Let's go.'

Spanton arose, and seemed relieved as he led the way around the house and walked to where the horses were waiting. Carson took a pair of handcuffs from his saddlebag and snapped them around Spanton's wrists. They rode out in the direction of Cattle Creek, and Carson pushed on fast, wanting to catch up with Pendle and Fargo before they could reach town.

He spotted the pair when they were about two miles from Cattle Creek, and warned Spanton to remain at his side. They soon overhauled Pendle and Fargo, and the couple, when they heard the sound of hooves at their backs, swung round and halted.

'Spanton!' exclaimed Fargo. 'Why've you left the ranch?'

Carson reined in, his right hand on the butt of his holstered sixgun. Spanton remained silent as he brought his horse to a halt, and Carson, watching Fargo, saw the man's cold eyes narrow as understanding began to get through to him.

'I'm the man you're riding into town to kill,' said Carson, 'and I figure you killed my brother, Lon

Carson.'

Fargo cursed as he reached for his gun, and he was fast. He cleared leather, at the same time diving sideways out of his saddle. But Carson was faster. He drew his Colt smoothly and waited for Fargo to hit the ground. Fargo landed on his feet, crouching as he brought up his gun, and Carson fired at the last possible moment, sending a .45 slug into the man's chest. The crash of the shot threw echoes clear to the horizon as gunsmoke flared.

Fargo's gun spilled from his hand. He slumped to the ground, and blood spread over the front of his shirt. He jerked spasmodically before relaxing in death. Carson thumbed back the hammer of his gun and turned the muzzle on the white-faced Pendle, who lifted his hands shoulder high.

'I ain't armed, Marshal,' Pendle said. 'I got nothin' to do with this.'

'You carried word to Mabry about his crooked business.' Carson's voice was harsh. 'You knew an attempt was made on my life in town this morning, and you're aware that Fargo was on his way to town kill me. That puts you right in the middle of it, and if you know what's good for you then start spillin' the beans.'

'Pendle, keep your trap shut,' rasped Spanton.

Carson swung his horse around and moved in against Spanton, his sixgun lifting fast. Spanton ducked, but the muzzle of the gun cracked against his right temple and he pitched sideways out of his saddle. Carson caught a furtive movement from the corner of his eye and turned swiftly in time to see Pendle pulling a small pistol out of his jacket pocket. Reacting instinctively, Carson thumbed a shot at the man, his horse still moving, and the bullet thudded into Pendle's right shoulder. Pendle fell forward over the neck of his horse and the startled animal bolted, heading along the trail to town. Pendle slipped sideways out of the saddle and hit the ground hard, landing on his head and bouncing a couple of times before lying inertly on his face.

Carson dismounted and went to Pendle's side. A sigh escaped him when he saw that the man was dead, his neck broken. He went back to Spanton, who was stirring, and pulled him to his feet, shaking him to bring him fully back to his senses.

'Who is Pendle?' Carson demanded. 'What does he do in town? How is he mixed up with Mabry?'

'Is Pendle dead?' Spanton demanded.

'As dead as Fargo,' Carson snapped.

'Pendle's got a wife and a couple of kids.' Spanton shook his head, badly shocked by the grim turn of events.

'He should have thought of that before pulling a gun on me.' Carson thrust Spanton back into his saddle and then mounted the black. He left the bodies on the trail, grasped Spanton's reins, and set a fast pace towards the town.

Cattle Creek looked deserted in the hot mid-morning sun, and Carson was sweating when he reined up at the hitch rail in front of the law office. He dragged Spanton out of his saddle and thrust him towards the door of the jail, which opened at their approach. Sheriff Rourke appeared in the doorway, his eyes narrowing when he saw the handcuffs on Spanton's wrists.

'Throw Spanton in a cell, Sheriff.' Carson thrust the man towards the law office. 'There are two men, Pendle and Fargo, dead on the trail about two miles out. Who is Pendle and what does he do around town?'

'Pendle? He's a clerk for Otto Kunkel,' gasped the sheriff. 'One of the quiet men around town.'

'He carried word of the attempt on my life to Mabry's place this morning.' Carson explained what had happened. 'You better ride out to Mabry's place and arrest him when he shows up there. Take a posse with you.'

Rourke shook his head as if unable to keep pace with the developments. He ushered Spanton into the cell block, and Carson followed and removed his cuffs from the prisoner. He looked at the other prisoners, who were silently watching, and saw Shap Newman glowering at him from a corner cell.

Carson glanced at Rourke. The sheriff seemed in no hurry to take a posse out after Mabry, and impatience filled Carson when he considered the sheriff's attitude since his arrival in town.

'Get a move on, Rourke,' he said. 'We need Mabry in jail.'

'Sure.' Rourke moved to the door. 'I'll take half a dozen men and ride out.' He departed quickly.

'Leave someone to guard this place,' Carson called after him. He left the office a moment later and walked along the street. Tiredness was clawing at his mind. He badly needed sleep but there was no time for that. He saw Rourke going along the sidewalk. The sheriff paused at the doorway of the store and spoke to someone inside, then continued. Carson followed, and as he passed the store Otto Kunkel appeared in the doorway. The big storekeeper's massive bulk filled the doorway, and he leaned against the door post.

'Is it true what I heard, Marshal?' Kunkel demanded.

'What did you hear?'

'Mabry is running the local rustling.'

'Who told you that?'

'The sheriff. I am the town mayor. I got a right to know these things.'

'Then Rourke told you right, and I figure the whole crooked business will come into the open now. Did Rourke tell you about your clerk?'

'Pendle.' Kunkel's tone was heavy. 'It's a bad business, Marshal. He leaves a wife and two children.'

'I'd like to know how he got mixed up in that business.' Carson studied Kunkel's fleshy face. 'Pendle was your clerk. How come he wasn't at the store this morning? Did you give him some time off?'

'He didn't come in this morning.' Kunkel shook his head. 'I got word he was sick.'

'I'll check that out later,' Carson promised. 'Who told you Pendle was sick?'

'His boy came in soon after I opened the store.' Kunkel shook his head. 'What is happening in this town, Marshal?'

'I don't know all of it yet but I'll get there. I got some prisoners in jail, and when they start talking it will all come out.'

He moved on, and, reaching the alley at the side of the store, paused and glanced along its dusty length. This was where Lon had been gunned down. He entered the alley and walked to the spot where his brother had fallen, looking around as if hoping the truth of what had happened would emerge and hit him in the face.

The sound of a window at his back creaking open cut through his thoughts and alarm flashed into his mind. Moving fast, he spun to face the sound, gun leaping into his hand. He saw the muzzle of a shotgun appearing in the aperture of a window in the store and sprang to the cover of the wall, shooting through the window. Quick gun blasts smashed out the silence and then the big figure of Otto Kunkel sprawled forward to crash through the window, the shotgun spilling from his nerveless hands to lie glinting ominously in the morning sunlight.

TWELVE

Carson stared at Kunkel, shocked by the development. The storekeeper had tried to kill him. What had precipitated his deadly action? Had he realized that with Pendle dead the truth of his own involvement might be revealed?

The sound of approaching footsteps jerked Carson from his thoughts and he glanced over his shoulder to see Sheriff Rourke entering the alley, gun in hand. He came to Carson's side, gazing at the big figure of the dead storekeeper draped over the window sill. The shotgun lying in the dust under the window was stark testimony to what had occurred.

'He tried to kill you!' exclaimed Rourke.

'Looks that way.' Carson drew a deep breath, then exhaled slowly. 'I guess he was mixed up in the crooked business, and Pendle getting killed must have backed him into a corner. Go and close the store. We'll need to check it for evidence. You got your posse together yet?'

'Yeah. They're getting their horses. I'll be riding out shortly.'

Carson walked out of the alley and Rourke followed him. A crowd was gathering on the sidewalk.

'I just seen Doc Hayman,' Rourke said. 'He wants a lawman present when he exhumes Lon's body today.'

Carson stiffened at the news, then nodded, recalling that he had asked the doctor to recover the bullet that killed Lon.

'I'll attend to the doctor,' he said. 'I'll see him shortly.'

'Then I'd better be riding now,' said Rourke.

'No. Wait,' Carson said. 'Let's look inside the store.'

Rourke followed him into the store. A clerk was standing behind the counter, serving a woman as if nothing untoward had occurred. The woman departed as Carson reached the counter, and the clerk eyed him uncertainly.

'Did Pendle report for work this morning?' Carson asked.

'Sure. He never missed a day's work in three years.'

'But he didn't work today,' Carson persisted. 'Were you here when he showed up?'

'Yep. Kunkel called him into the office, and five minutes later Pendle left the store. I ain't seen him since.'

Carson nodded, and motioned for Rourke to follow him into Kunkel's office. At that moment Doc Hayman called to him from the street door, and came to the office.

'I just heard that Kunkel has been killed,' said the doc. 'Who did it?'

'I did.' Carson shook his head. 'Take a look at the body. We'll need to keep the record straight.'

They crowded into the office. Rourke and Hayman pulled Kunkel's body off the window sill and laid it out on the floor. Hayman carried out a swift examination.

'Killed by a single shot to the heart,' he pronounced. 'The entry wound was made by a .45 slug, I'd say.'

'You're right,' Carson nodded. 'Take a look out the window and you'll see the shotgun he meant to turn loose on me. I need to establish that killing him was self defence.'

Hayman leaned over the bloodstained sill and peered into the alley. 'It's a clear cut case,' he said.

Carson looked at the big iron safe standing against the back wall of the office, its door ajar.

'Witness my actions, Rourke.' Carson crossed to the safe and pulled the door open wide. There were ledgers and papers on the top shelf, and wads of paper money, neatly bundled, on the lower shelf. A drawer was situated under the bottom shelf and Carson pulled it open to reveal wads of notes stacked neatly inside. The notes were new, contained in wrappers.

'Hey, that looks like the dough from the Prescott bank!' Rourke exclaimed. 'It was robbed a few weeks ago! What's that dough doing here?'

Carson picked up one of the wads of paper money and read the details stamped on the wrapper. 'I happened to be by the stable when Mabry rode in the night before last with Wiley and Raynor,' he mused. 'Mabry told his men he was gonna see the boss. No name was mentioned so I followed him for a spell. He went to the law office and spoke to you, Rourke, then saw Kunkel in here.'

'There's the tie-in,' said Rourke. 'You sure made things hum when you showed up.'

'Let's go talk to the prisoners,' Carson decided. 'Have you finished in here, Doc?'

'Sure thing,' Hayman nodded. 'I'll need a lawman to attend the exhumation I'm gonna do on your brother this morning.'

'I'll accompany you,' Carson said.

Hayman shook his head. 'I would advise you against it. Rourke can officiate. I've sent two men out to the graveyard to open up the grave. Be ready to accompany me in thirty minutes, Sheriff.'

'I got to leave in a hurry,' Rourke protested.

'I need you as a witness. Be at my office in thirty minutes.' Doc Hayman closed and bolted the window. 'Better lock this place up tight,' he advised.

Carson nodded. He locked the safe and then the office as they left. Ordering the clerk to leave, he locked the store and walked to the jail with Rourke accompanying him.

'Bring Wiley out of the cells,' Carson said. 'I wanta put pressure on him, and he looks the type to crack.'

Rourke fetched Wiley from the cells. The gunman looked sullen when he was ushered into the office. Carson made him sit down, then stood over him.

'You're in a heap of trouble, Wiley,' he said harshly. 'I've been finding out a few things about the crookedness that's been going on around here and your name has come up several times. Otto Kunkel is dead. He tried to gun me down in the alley where my brother was shot. The sheriff is about to take a posse out to arrest Mabry. I just searched Kunkel's safe and found the money that was stolen from the bank in Prescott a few weeks ago. Mabry organised the bank raid, and you were in on it.'

'That ain't so.' Wiley started to his feet and Rourke slammed him back into his seat. 'I ain't taking the blame for something I wasn't in on,' he rasped. 'The banker was killed on that raid, and I ain't gonna hang for something I didn't do.'

'Then you better come clean and help the law.' Carson spoke firmly. 'Give me the lowdown on what's been going on and if you didn't take part in the bank raid I'll see you get leniency when you come to trial.'

'Mabry handled it.' Wiley spoke without hesitation. 'He told me about it afterwards. Mabry killed the banker, and passed the bank money to Kunkel. Mabry and Kunkel were working hand in hand. Ask Talman. He can back me up. He's Mabry's right hand.'

'Fetch Talman.' Carson glanced at Rourke, who went into the cell block.

Talman's fleshy face wore an expression of defiance when he entered the office. He paused in the doorway and Rourke shoved him from behind.

'Cut out the rough stuff,' Talman snarled, turning to face Rourke, and the sheriff slammed his left fist into Talman's face, knocking him to the floor. Talman scrambled up, cursing.

'Sit down and keep your mouth shut until you're spoken to,' Carson rapped. 'Tell me about the bank raid in Prescott. You were in on it, and a bank man was killed.'

Talman turned on Wiley. 'You been opening your trap?'

'Whaddya think I'm gonna do, take the rap for you and Mabry?' demanded Wiley. 'I ain't mixed up in murder and bank robbery.'

'What about the rustling at Double J? You was in on that for sure,' Talman countered.

Wiley shook his head. 'I didn't ride on that one. I was sick at the time.'

'Who killed my brother Lon, and why was he shot?' cut in Carson.

'You trying to pin that on me?' Talman stared defiantly at Carson. 'I ain't Mabry.'

'Mabry?' Carson stiffened. 'What happened?'

'Gimme a deal and I'll tell you.' Talman grinned. 'I sure ain't taking the rap for anyone. You put in a good word for me with the judge and I'll spill the beans. Wiley can't tell you anything. He wasn't in with Mabry like me.'

'Keep talking,' said Carson. 'Give me information I can use and if I find you weren't involved I'll see you get leniency.'

'Mabry killed your brother because he was getting too nosey about the crooked business being run around here. Johnson told your brother someone had been rolled for his dough in the alley beside Kunkel's store, and when your brother went to investigate, Mabry shot him in the back from Kunkel's office window. I heard Kunkel and Mabry talking it over earlier that evening, and next morning I heard your brother was killed exactly like that. Is that enough proof for you?'

'Will you repeat that in court?' Carson demanded.

'Sure. I ain't gonna take a murder rap for anyone.'

'Put them back where they belong,' Carson said to Rourke. 'They'll keep until I get back. Talman, I'm gonna check out your story, and it better be true.'

'It's the truth,' Talman insisted as he and Wiley were returned to the cells.

Carson was lost in thought until Rourke returned to the office, jangling the big bunch of keys in his hand.

'What happens now?' Rourke asked. 'Looks like you got all the proof you need.'

'See Doc Hayman and tell him to put off the exhumation on my brother until I've checked out Talman's story,' Carson said. 'I'll stick around in the office until you get back. Then I'd better ride out with your posse to pick up Mabry. I want him behind bars.' He paused, then said: 'Where's Dora Hand? I left her in here yesterday in protective custody?'

'Norton said she was in the spare room,' Rourke said. 'I ain't seen her myself.'

He departed, and Carson went into the cell block and stood for a moment looking at the prisoners. Wiley and Talman were together in one cell and two of the three men Mabry had sent into town to spring the prisoners loose were in another. Newman was sitting alone in a third cell.

Carson left the cell block and locked the door. As he dropped the keys on the desk the street door opened and Rourke entered, carrying a shotgun under his arm. He lifted the gun and covered Carson, his rugged face grim.

'I ain't warned the posse to ride out,' he said. 'And I ain't about to arrest Mabry. I threw in with him a long time ago so I've got to kill you, Carson. You're the only one who knows what's been goin' on, and with you dead and the prisoners escaped from jail no one will know who killed you and that will be the end of it.'

'So that's the way of it!' Carson nodded. 'I've had doubts about you all along.' His right hand was down at his side, but as fast as he was with a gun he knew he could not beat the sheriff. The knuckle of Rourke's trigger finger was white under the pressure he was exerting upon it and the twin muzzles of the fearsome weapon were gaping at Carson's chest.

'I'll see that you get buried beside your brother,' Rourke said. 'Now get back into the cells and turn the prisoners loose. You're gonna die a hero's death, killed trying to stop a jail break.'

Carson picked up the keys and walked towards the connecting door. Rourke followed, prodding him between the shoulder blades with the shotgun, and the instant that the twin barrels touched him, Carson pivoted to his left on heel and toe, his left arm lifting to make contact with the long barrel of the shotgun and sweeping outwards to divert the muzzle from his body. He drew his gun in a lightning fast movement, and at that moment he heard the street door opening.

Cal Mabry was entering the office, and the outlaw took in the situation at a glance. His right hand dropped quickly to the butt of his holstered gun. Carson thumbed back the hammer of his Colt as it lifted to cover Rourke. The sheriff was trying to back off and gain room to bring his shotgun to bear. Carson realized he was running out of time and pressed the muzzle of his sixgun against Rourke's chest and squeezed the trigger.

The Colt blasted deafeningly and the sheriff jerked under the impact of the big slug. Carson dropped to one knee as the sheriff fell to the floor, swinging his gun to cover Mabry, who was lifting his Colt into action. The outlaw fired swiftly and his bullet plunked through the crown of Carson's Stetson. Carson flipped his gun into line with Mabry's big body and triggered fast, narrowing his eyes against flaring gunsmoke. Mabry got off a second shot, which smashed into Carson's left shoulder, and then Carson's slugs hammered into Mabry's chest. The outlaw dropped his gun and followed it to the floor, blood spurting from his neck to form a gory pool on the pine boards.

The heavy detonations of the shooting faded slowly and Carson staggered back against the door leading into the cells. His right hand dropped to his side, still gripping his smoking gun, and he gritted his teeth against the wave of pain that surged through his shoulder. He lifted the gun, thumbed the hammer to half-cock, opened the loading gate and stuffed fresh shells into the used chambers. Lowering the hammer on an empty chamber, he holstered the weapon, his thoughts slow.

He staggered out to the sidewalk, breathing deeply of the clean air. Townsmen were coming along the street from all directions, attracted by the shooting, and he saw Doc Hayman in the lead. He sat down on the edge of the sidewalk and leaned his head against a post. His ears were singing from the detonations of the shooting, and he yawned to clear them. Silence was returning and he nodded, for silence meant that the guns had finished talking and his problems were over.